MAR 1 5 2023

Ode to a Nobody

CAROLINE BROOKS DUBOIS

HOLIDAY HOUSE · NEW YORK

Holiday House / New York

Copyright © 2022 by Caroline Brooks DuBois

All Rights Reserved

HOLIDAY HOUSE is registered in the U.S. Patent and Trademark Office.

Printed and bound in September 2022 at Maple Press, York, PA, USA.

www.holidayhouse.com

First Edition

1 3 5 7 9 10 8 6 4 2

Library of Congress Cataloging-in-Publication Data

Names: DuBois, Caroline Brooks, author.

Title: Ode to a nobody / Caroline Brooks DuBois.

Description: First edition. | New York : Holiday House, [2022] | Audience:
  Ages 8-12. | Audience: Grades 4-6. | Summary: After a devastating
  tornado tears apart her home, thirteen-year-old Quinn struggles to find
  stability and return to who she was before, finding she has to rebuild
  herself.

Identifiers: LCCN 2022002950 | ISBN 9780823451562 (hardcover)

Subjects: CYAC: Novels in verse. | Resilience (Personality trait)— Fiction.
  Identity—Fiction. | Families—Fiction. | LCGFT: Novels in verse.

Classification: LCC PZ7.5.D83 Od 2022 | DDC [Fic]—dc23

LC record available at https://lccn.loc.gov/2022002950

To East Nashville, with love.

And to my students, for inspiration.

Ode to a Nobody

The Before

EXPERT OF NOTHING

It's another Monday
and I'm still the student
I was on Friday. Worse,
my pencil's gone dumb in my grip
and I begin to sweat.
I head my paper *Quinnie*.
Easy enough! Deep breath.
Erase that, write *Quinn*.
Erase that, write *Quinn(ie)*.
Erase that—and rip
a jagged hole in my paper
that I want to slip
in-
to.

Ms. Koval eyes me, says,
"Don't think too hard.
Just make a list
of everything you're good at,
or consider yourself
an expert on."

My page is empty,
like my mind.
Maybe I should write
Good at sweating.
Everyone else is hunched,
madly writing—like way more
than usual. Even Jack
across the room tosses
words onto his paper.
Of course! He's an expert skater,
gamer, and talker—
when he's in trouble.

Maybe I should write
Good for nothing.

"You can refer to this list
when you need
a topic for a poem."

Two rows in front of Jack
sits Jade, who turned our friend group
from two to three last year
when she came here
from another school.
She flips to the back
of her paper and keeps going.
Also an expert skater—
all tricks and skill—

an expert rule breaker,
expert at being the new
girl in middle school,
expert at befriending
Jack—and me, I guess.
I was the plastic toy
chucked in for free.

My paper waits
impatiently
for my expertise.

"Three more minutes,"
Ms. Koval says.

I pop my knuckles.
If I were Forrest,
I'd write *perfect student, valedictorian, prototypical son.*
Basically, a chameleon.
No joke—he aces everything.
He's even supreme
as a brother.

When it comes to me,
I'm coming up empty.
How will I start this project
if I can't even start
this list?

I stare out the window
at a kite caught in the power lines.
I think about my Cs,
the F I've got in math,
and a B in English just 'cause
Ms. Koval is kind.

I write on my paper:
I'm a kite dangling from a branch,
tangled and tossing
in the shadows
of tall trees.

Not bad, I think.

"Prepare to partner-share
your areas of expertise,"
Ms. Koval says. I gulp,
erase, quick-scribble:
>*decent caretaker of small animals*
>*basic skater*
>*competent gamer*

Maybe with practice,
I can become
an expert at one
of these.

MOM THOUGHT I WAS GOING TO BE A BOY

Today in English,
we're writing our origin stories
in fifteen sentences or fewer.
This I think I can manage.
Mine goes:

Mom's ultrasound and intuition
convinced her
I was to be born a boy.
So my parents chose a name
and for nine long months
called me *Quinn*.

When I turned out a girl,
Mom still liked Quinn.
"It's gender-neutral,"
she insisted.

Dad disagreed
and has always called me
Quinnie. So it's *Quinn* on paper,
but out loud mostly *Quinnie*
and sometimes *Quinn*,
depending on
who's speaking.

Quinn(ie) Jolene Nash—
is how I've been writing it lately,
so neither parent
can claim me as their victory.
That's me.
Age thirteen.
Master of nothing.

Mom got to name me.
Essentially, she won:
Dad zip, Mom one
in case anyone's keeping score.
I know *they* are!

Sometimes when she calls me,
I wonder if she wishes
I'd been born that boy,
or some other version
who doesn't mess up
so much.

PUMPKIN'S ORIGIN STORY

Last summer, Mom and Dad
were exchanging words—not kind ones.
And Forrest said, "Let's go!" We hopped in his car,
windows down, music up. He took me to Pet Town.
"Pretty sure they don't take sisters," I told him.

"Not even pesky ones?" His smile always made things okay.
We strolled the aisles. Named all the kittens. Then
we noticed him, or maybe Pumpkin picked us.
Standing on his hind legs, nose wiggling, whiskers working,
a hamster round like a pumpkin. "Should we ask Mom?"
"Nah," Forrest said, "we got this." He paid, carried
the cage, and helped me set Pumpkin up
in my bedroom. "Now you have a four-footed
friend to talk to." Forrest was right:
Pumpkin's made for listening—
always here, and all ears.

FREEWRITE

"Freewriting is the warm-up,"
Ms. Koval pep-talks, "before
the big game," before
we "kick off" the April
poetry project.

Jade would call this busywork.

Jack would say it's just another teacher
preaching how words hold the power
to shape our lives—
or a teacher trick so she can pick
the shiniest students to read
at the End-of-Year Coffeehouse
for the smiling parents.

I can picture it:
Jack and me in the back row,
feet kicked up on another desk,
some brainiac mumbling poems
from their polished portfolio.
            But for a split second, I picture
myself up there.

Reality check:
if this is the warm-up
before the game, I will
be the one warming the bench.
No medals, ribbons, or plaque
for my wall.

            Mom and Dad
will be relieved
if I at least pull a C.

ACROSTIC ASSIGNMENT: WHAT'S IN A NAME?

Questioning.
Untalented? A blunder? I wonder:
If my brother's star beams bright, does it
Nullify my dull speck of light?
Not trying to compete with *his* glory.
(In this lifetime.
End of story.)

FRIENDLY FEEDBACK

You wrote on my acrostic
in teacher cursive and teacher ink:
I bet there's more to your story.
But what if my story is boring?
What if I'm not the appetizer, main course,
or dessert, but the leftovers—cold hamburger
missing its bun in the back of the fridge,
two sprigs of broccoli, and a stale biscuit?
What if I'm just another kid in this class
clumped with "those" kids in the back,
the ones you keep an eye on, taking notes.
What if my brother, who you taught
and called "brilliant"—as if I didn't know—
is the better model? Sounds about right,
since he got the better version
of my parents too.

SIMILE ASSIGNMENT: "WRITING IS LIKE . . ."

Writing is like homework—
but it beats math any day.
I won't say *homefun.*
No thanks, Ms. Koval,
for that pun, because
it's still hard and I can't
figure it out. At least

with math, it's right or wrong.
And mostly wrong—if you're me.

If writing were like skating,
I'd say *Skate on!*
and attempt to be boss,
with Jack and Jade
my audience.

If writing were like gaming,
I'd say *Game on!* and try
to win. But it's not. And I haven't
beat Jack or Jade at a game
in weeks.

If I were a real writer,
I'd win contests, glow in applause.
Not be here writing this poemful of flaws,
while Jack and Jade are out somewhere
having fun. If words flowed freely,
this would be easy. But I'm not,
and they don't.

Writing is like a job,
serious work putting thoughts into words.
Just sitting and thinking, just penning—
no high score to beat, no next level to reach,
so how will anyone know
if I'm winning?

Honestly, I have no clue
what writing is like, or how
to do this simile assignment correctly—
          but it feels like something
I can kinda wing
from beginning to end.
So maybe poetry
is like an opportunity.
If I turn each poem in,
you'll see I'm trying here
and give me a B.

MORE FEEDBACK

This time, you wrote
Yes, it's something you can do!
Next time, don't focus so much
on rhyming—or your grade.

But a poem without rhyme sounds dumb.

You also wrote *Poetry is about possibilities, not limitations.*

But the grades on my report card
tell a different story.

You said I'm almost ready for the project
but in the next poem I should *loosen up a bit.*

These March practice poems
you keep assigning
with syllable
and word counts
are so confining
that my thoughts don't fit.

CINQUAIN ASSIGNMENT: AKA

Gamertag
Player, Sister
Skating, Gaming, (Writing?)
Sometimes Known Online As
Quinn(ie)

A SECRET

"What are we supposed
to write about?" Jade grumps
to Ms. Koval and the class
during *quiet writing time.*

"About yourself, Jade.
Stuff you know or care about,
want to explore
or think about."

Jack joins in, "Like mac-n-cheese
or clean underwear?"

Ms. Koval takes a deep breath.
"You may write about whatever you like,
as long as you write a poem
each day in April. And—
I'll tell you a secret."

I put down my pencil and look up,
skeptical but hopeful—
always on the hunt for shortcuts,
clues to everyone
else's success.

She looks us over evenly,
lowers her voice, and whispers,
"A poet once wrote,
'No man is an island.'"*

I sigh at the riddle
and look back down.

Then she says, "Everything
is connected, and everything has a voice.
Writers must listen and observe—
and then poems happen.

"I'm not saying,
Jack and Jade, you'll literally hear
objects talking to you." She adds
dramatically, "But I'm not
saying you won't either."

An uncomfortable laugh
spreads across the class
at our babbling teacher.

*John Donne

"WHATCHA DOING?"

Jack asks me
later during study hall,
which is our school home base,
last period of the day.
"Nothing," I say, and quick-shut
my English notebook.

"For a minute,
I thought you were studying—
or listening for stuff
to start talking to you."

"Nope," I say, and stash
my notebook in my locker,
while Jade and Jack crack

each other up saying,
Leaves are people too.
And trees.
And bees.

Study hall is for studying.
Or if you're Jack, Jade, and me—
time for talking, because Mr. Slade
is mega-cool
with whatever we do,
as long as "you keep your butts
in your seats" during the end-of-day
announcements.

HOMEWORK: DIAMANTE "OPPOSITES"

Stuck Between a Diamond and a Stone
By Quinn(ie)

Mom
Artsy, Citified
Shopping, Networking, Self-Improving
Starbucks, Malls, Meadows, Creeks
Hiking, Building, Nature-Blogging
Rustic, Countrified
Dad

"WHO WILL READ THEIR OPPOSITES POEM?"

In English, when three kids share their poems
out loud with the class—two featuring
their moms and dads—Jack makes a ball
of his poem and three-point swishes it
from his desk into the trash.
I whisper-shout *Score!* and he gives me
a classic Jack grin.

Ms. Koval says calmly, "Jack."
And holds up two fingers
for a *Second warning!*

"Who cares if she calls my mom?"
Jack practically spits after class.

I know
he cares.
I wonder if Ms. Koval knows.
Jade appears
between us: "Yeah, who cares!"
She agrees with Jack.
"I wrote about winners
and losers. Losers
write poems about
their parents."

I flash back
to a time before Jade—
Jack and I readying a sled
at the top of a snowy hill
in City Park—maybe age seven or eight.
I am frozen in fear, until he takes
my mittened hand
and shouts, "Together, we
conquer this hill!"
And we did.

I look at him now in the hall.
All limbs. Sprouting hair
on his upper lip.
He feels me staring
and insists, "No
                    big
                            deal!"

I nod to let him know I hear.

"Poetry's stupid anyway," Jade says.

Jack smirks. "Watch this!"
and drop-kicks his backpack
into our next class.

Jade bends in half laughing.

I do the same thing
with my backpack
just to win
Jack's smile again.

Mr. Slade tells us,
"Go back out
and try coming in
again."

AFTER SCHOOL, JUST JACK & ME

"What should we do?"
Jack asks, even though the answer
is usually skate.

If Jack says jump, you jump,
Mom likes to say.

We're on our boards—
hair flying, breeze prickling skin,
colors scrolling, cars beeping and zooming.
Jack whizzes past four kids playing
foursquare. I shoot through too.
I attempt an ollie and land it.
"Yes!" Jack shouts over
his shoulder.

I feel a rush of pride,
which triggers a memory
of Forrest's graduation party
last spring. Presents piled high,
with my brother the center of the universe,
as usual. Congratulations, hugs, and high fives
from guests, pushing me right out of the picture
and onto the back porch—where nobody
missed me. Jack came out and sat
down. "Big deal," he said,
"he graduated. Can't help
his birth order. Besides, he can't
even ollie, like you and me."

I smile goofily, skating
and reliving this memory.

Jack looks back at me now.
I focus, to navigate
the cracks and bumps
on the sidewalk of this new route
Jack's taking. He stops and pops
his board up. We're
across the street from City Park
and its yap-happy dog run.

"What's so funny?" he asks
as we watch and wait for
the traffic to clear.

"Just imagining Forrest on a board."

"Awkward," he agrees.

"Why'd we stop here?"
We're in front of an old house,
the one we habitually avoid.

Shrouded in shrubs and rumor,
the two-story seems to lean, as if tired.
Its yard, an urban jungle, smells
of mushrooms. All the other houses
that surround the park behave
and keep themselves
well groomed.

"You scared of this dump?" Jack asks,
then turns and faces the house.
He picks up a stick, wields it, and begins
to scratch at the historic marker
that climbs with vines at the edge
of the yard. I wince
and glance around. "Come on,"
I tell him, "let's go!"

"Be my lookout!"
He scuffs hard at the letters,
changing it from *Ivy Manor*
to *Ivy Man*.

I keep watch for him—because
that's what he'd do for me.

The only sound, other than
cars zipping past,
is a lone dog barking
from somewhere deep
within the overgrown property.

"Traffic's clear NOW," I call—
and Jack drops the stick.

We skate across the street to the park,
where we find a bench
and collapse into fits
of laughter (him) and relief (me)—
but I'm distracted—
looking back
at the house
and feeling like
it's looking
at me.

POEMING VS. GAMING

In class today,
we read odes.
In one, this dude Neruda*

praised his socks,
and across the room,
Jack scoffed, head-
planted his desk.
I stopped highlighting
to look up and agree
with my own two
rolling eyes.

Jack is right—
who writes a poem
about socks! Why not
a million dollars
or the moon? Or how
about that tree
outside my window?
Been staring at it
my whole life.

Jack would say,
Trees are dumb!
Stop poeming.
Start gaming.
Jack's voice
in my head
right now, his three-
word message
on my screen:
What's new, Q?

*Pablo Neruda's "Ode to My Socks"

ODE TO THE DOGWOOD OUT MY WINDOW

Trees are just there.
Like birds. Like air.
Except this one,
snuggled up close
to my house,
its branches stretching
and reaching

and

tap
      tap
           tapping

its tree fingers
against my pane
in the spring wind,
like a friend
come to rescue
me from
them
and all their yelling
downstairs.

IN TUNE

Like a sister-brother duet,
one memory
goes a little something like this:
Forrest trumpeting on the back porch—
because why would he practice indoors,
when all the world could hear?
Me sitting down beside him,
tapping his shoulder
until he pauses.
"Yes?"
"Just listening."
Him resuming.
Me tapping.
Him stopping.
"I'm practicing."
"Got a parade
or concert
or something?"
Him sighing.
Me tapping.
"I think you should play louder—
not *all* the dogs are howling."
"Funny, Quinnie. I can play quietly
if I want to."
Me grinning.
Him head-shaking.
"Fine, go on—
toot your own horn."

WORD DOC.

So here goes nothing.
"Write what you know,"
Ms. Koval says. So here I go,
but this is for my eyes alone.
O Word doc. on my laptop,
     I create, title, and save thee:
     QUINN(IE)'S Eighth-Grade PROJECT of Poetry.
     I shall blank-stare at you—
     white page of "opportunity,"
     white page glaring back at me.
     I shall minimize you. And game,
     with you in the background,
     try to beat Jack's high score
     to win his mad respect. O Word
     doc., I'll tackle you later, when
     inspiration smacks me, when
     Forrest's framed award-winning
     essay hanging in the hallway
     stops boasting and echoing
     and praising itself in my head—
     and when my own words
                 show up.
O Word doc., you're still here?
     Your tab open and waiting.
     The rubric says *One-a-Day*
     for an A starting this week. O Word doc.,
     I ask this of thee: Do you know

a website that will compose
thirty poems for me, for free?
        Nope. Trash. Delete. Delete. Delete!
Rhyming's not gonna be my thing.
"Freewrite, don't censor yourself,"
Ms. Koval explained, so here I go:
Starting over. Take two! I'll squeeze
my thinking into these short lines,
or "line breaks." Sprinkle in a dash
of simile&metaphor like cheese
atop this poemy mixture of words
& thoughts, since nothing real
is hitting me. "Begin new stanzas
like paragraphs," Ms. Koval says,
when you have a new idea or shift
in time or place or point of view.

                No new ideas here!
                But I've had shifts for sure,
                shifts for days,
                like the shift in my friendship
                to make room for Jade,
not SHIFT on the keyboard,
but shifts in place—Forrest shifted
from home to a dorm—and left me.
And now Dad is trying to ever-so-shiftily
shift right on out of here,
                as if Mom and I won't even notice.

CITY MOUSE, COUNTRY MOUSE—AND ME

The back door's closing right now.
Dad's exiting again; his parting words:
     "Only a few more nights out there."

But Mom and I aren't there.

     "Time crawls in the country," he says.

Time without us.

He has a good excuse to leave,
since his mom, Grandma Jo, is sick.
He sleeps in her spare bedroom,
his old room, to watch over her,
which is a good-son thing to do.
Leaving Mom and me alone,
her cue to retreat into her work,
in our city house, with Forrest away
and Dad playing country mouse.

Maybe Dad's been leaving all along,
trying to get back to the farm, where
he was born & raised. Mom convinced
him to settle here, after college.
But like her, I'm all city,
don't think twice about catching a bus,
hanging at City Park. Its benches,
my couches. Its trees and fountain,

my stomping ground. Dad inhabits
the country in his head, even when
he's with us. You can't help it
when you grow up a farm kid, cows
and chickens and all that fresh air.

"So peaceful out there—cricket-song and stars."

Mom prefers the city noise, a symphony.
          But for a country guy,
          he sure can phone-stare, get possessed
by his screen, like the rest of us.

INCLEMENT WEATHER DRILL IN STUDY HALL

On the floor! Face the wall!
On your knees. Heads down!

The assistant principal clacks past
us in the hall in her heels,
walkie-talkie on her hip.
Nothing says April Fools' about her.

No talking! Or we'll do it all over!

Somehow Jade
finds her way between Jack
and me on the floor. "Scooch,"

she commands, and I scooch
so she can squeeze her tan, athletic legs
and curving body between us.
Jack pops his head up to notice.

Jade is somehow all girl AND
just one of the guys at the same time.

Hands behind your heads!
The assistant principal warns us.

But the teachers can't maintain order
when someone farts
and chaos and laughter ripple
the eighth grade like a weather
pattern across
                    the
                        midstate.

SCHOOL RULES, ACCORDING TO JACK

Always,
go for the laugh!
Get noticed.
Do what it takes.
If you get in trouble—
it's still worth it.
Always!

MY PHILOSOPHY

One day, I might ask Forrest to read
these "poems"—
if they count as poems—
but probably not,
'cause he's forgotten about me, at college
in the green state of North Carolina.
On scholarship! With his near-perfect ACT.
Wake Forest—can you believe that?
Forrest, the talent of the family,
goes off to a college with his own name.
How poetic! And me, Quinn or Quinn(ie),
at home without a name of my own.
"Quinn," Mom calls, "have you seen
your dad?" Dad calls, "Quinnie, tell your
mom I left." And Forrest—he never calls.

When Forrest moved out last fall,
all the spoken words, the happy words,
whooshed out the windows and doors
with him, like a vacuum. Mom and Dad
type their words into their phones
or laptops, or spit and sling them
into the air at each other, while I duck.

Forrest, who's studying philosophy,
was home briefly at Christmas and said,

"I think; therefore I am."
That's philosophy for *I exist*.
But he also said, "I'm outta here!"
when the yelling got started
and Dad stomped away from Mom
to Grandma Jo's—and my words
got lost in all the chaos. You,
O Word doc., could be a record of me,
my important thoughts, so *therefore, I am*.
I still exist, even if
Forrest left me to sop up
our broken bowl of parental mess.

That makes me think, Ms. Koval,
of that saying that I just Googled:
"You cannot see the forest for the trees."
But in my case, "You cannot see me
for the Forrest," because everyone
always sees Forrest; it's me,
Quinn(ie), no one sees.

NATIONAL POETRY MONTH

Also known as April
Also known as the month of showers that bring May flowers
and pollen and sneezing and bee stings and state assessments
Also known as the month my teachers ask me
to rescue my grades from the trash can
Also known as Forrest's birthday month
Where mine occurs on exactly one day in August,

Forrest's has been known to last for days—
his college friends are probably celebrating him,
while I'm a party-of-one stuck at home
Apparently, April has more cons than pros
"A whole month of poetry," Jack groans
in English. But I'm curious, because
April needs a serious reboot.

ODE TO A STATIONARY OLLIE

Back foot pops
the tail of your board
                        down,

while front foot scoops
                                                air
                                    into
                            up
                    board
        the

Leaving ground—
board and skater united as one!
(At least that's how it's supposed to work!)

ODE TO MY BEDROOM (AND PUMPKIN)

My place of escape.
Not a square inch of white wall showing.
Posters mostly, and a shrine of Pumpkin pictures. My computer,
with the Lego girl on a skateboard Jack gave me posing on top.
Pumpkin's smelly cage on my dresser, his wheel going round
and round. My bed, the comforter's yellow sunshine
and pillows every color of the rainbow, sheets so cloud-soft
I could sleep forever, close my eyes and burrow under
when there's fighting downstairs. Or turn up my music,
put my headphones on, stare out the window
at the dogwood tree Dad planted when I was born
to grow along with me, keep me company.
My bedroom, my bedroom.
My place of escape.

WHEN FORREST LEFT FOR SCHOOL LAST AUGUST

Things changed.
I don't know who
or what to blame.
Things just changed.

He drove away
waving, looking
like someone
who knows

who they are
and where
they're going.

Mom picked
up the house
afterward.
Dad cried
and sat in Forrest's
room. One of them
downstairs,
the other
upstairs—and me
sitting on the stairs
in between.

"QUINNIE SAYS"

Like the game Simon Says,
Forrest used to say "Quinnie Says"
when I was little. He likes to tell me,
"Before you could walk, you'd point
with your stubby finger, and we'd bring you
whatever you wanted—
just to shut you up."

We had our own version of the game.
I'd say, "Quinnie says *Stop reading*,"

and he'd dog-ear his page.

I'd say, "Quinnie says *Tickle me*,"
and he'd put down his homework.

I'd say, "Quinnie says *Sing to me*,"
and he'd get off his phone.

I'd say, "Quinnie says *Read me a book*,"
and he would.

      He always did
whatever I said
when I said it
like that.

IF THEN

If Forrest was the glue
binding the family
then I am the heat
weakening the bond.

If Forrest was the duct tape,
the button, the magnet, the bungee
holding us together,
then I am the resistance,
the yank, the pull.

If Forrest was the paper clip
filing us together as four,
then I am the paper slipped
to the floor.

If Forrest is the needle
threading our family
quilt with game nights,
chess & Monopoly
& made-up traditions,
then I am the tear
and rip, the "not
tonight."

I
am a game of
solitaire.

ME TIME

I thought they'd be all mine,
their focus flooding down on me, the second-born;
it's more like a trickle or a spurt. Maybe
I like it like that. It equates to more hang time
with Jack and Jade. Set me up with my computer,
a bag of Doritos, bowl of gummy bears,
and I'm set for the day. No one monitoring
my "screen time," or where I go.

These days, Mom's busy on her laptop, and Dad's
penning *Woodsy,* his nature blog, on his phone.
So I'm on my own—and nobody cares.

Until I'm paged:
"Quinn, come downstairs!"

"It's Forrest on the phone!" Mom waves me over,
all smiles and fanfare for him.

I pop up in the video's background, say *hi.*

Forrest talks about his classes, dorm news,
the gobs of friends he's made.
It's always been about him.
He forgets to ask how I am or how it's been—
or maybe he doesn't want to ask in front of Mom.
So it's *adiós* from me and back up to my queendom,
my cave, my bedroom, for more
unadulterated ME time.

BACKSTORY OF BEST FRIEND JACK

Our moms met, as they tell us,
colliding, one stroller—BAM—into
the other. Me sobbing
and Jack giggling & pointing.

Best friends ever since!
                      Since before
we could walk, or talk, before
we could skate, or game. First—
daycare together, then preschool,
elementary, and now middle
school across town.

Jack is exactly half
a year older than me.
As an infant, I followed him.
He took his first step—and Mom said
I pulled up just to seize the block
in his hand. "President, secretary,
treasurer, and founding member
of the Jack Fan Club," she calls me.
"If Jack said jump off a moving bike, Quinn,
you would." In fact, one day, Jack
told me to jump off my house.
Guess what? I did, and sprained my ankle.
Ended up with a cast that Jack
drew jokes and pictures all over.

Picture him like this: a mullet,
because he couldn't decide—short or long.
Baggy shorts year-round, and solid tees,
mostly black. And always, always
the camo jacket his dad gave him

before he left.
Once, I saw him sleep in it. And one
time, when he thought he lost it,
he moped for two weeks.

His mom, June,
is a nurse who's "getting out there,"
which according to Jack
means meeting bald men
on dating apps.

(Ms. Koval, he wouldn't like me writing his secrets,
so please don't read this aloud to the class.)

Jack taught me all the skate tricks I know,
which is exactly two and counting:
a stationary and a moving ollie.
But I'm getting better,
catching up to Jack and Jade.
Jack also taught me to defend myself
when a high schooler snatched my phone
on the bus. Jack said, "Cool move. Now give it
back, dude." And dude did—not because Jack's bigger
or taller, but because he's Jack.

Like,
I could have my hand up for ages
and teachers will still call on him,
doodling on his desk, and his answer

will sound legit. Not gonna lie.
He's super talented like that.
He's Jack.

FAVORITES

Jack's include
spicy mac-n-cheese,
his duct-taped board,
and his camo jacket.

I wonder
>   *Can he name mine?*

>   *Can I?*

A few weeks ago,
I missed a day of school
and Jack switched desks in English
to sit beside Jade.

Jade, with her blond braids
& waist-tied flannels,
T-shirts that read
Skate like a girl!
and
Sister Skatehood.

A year ago,
when she transferred in—
all loud-talking and upbeat mood,
banged-up skater knees
and elbows—we were
mega-impressed,
especially Jack.
We appointed her
our *favorite*
at-school friend.

Lately, I wonder
who his favorite
is now.

CITY GAMES

On our way home from school
on the city bus, I tell Jack,
"Dad's gone to the country again."
"Gone granola," he adds without a beat,
which makes me smile.

Maybe because I'm talking about *my dad,*
when *his* phone chimes,
he does a wild dance move to dig it
out of his backpack in time.

Everyone knows
when it's a number you don't recognize,
you don't answer.
But Jack always does.

"Hello?

Hello?

Hello?"

I hear the hope in his voice,
cross my fingers behind my back,
then watch his face fall.

When he tosses his phone back in his pack,
I ask him quietly, "You okay?"

"Never better," he says.
And I almost believe him.

Then he struts to the front of the bus
bopping the back of every kid's head.
He turns and smirks at me.
I give my *Jack, shape up!* look.

He shrugs and comes back,
fake high-fives me,
and then plops back down
beside me.

We jump off the bus
a few stops before ours
to stand on the interstate overpass,
watching cars like sport, the hypnotizing zip
as they pass below us, the warm gust
up and over the bridge.

Jack shouts, "Top of the world!"

I shout, "Top of the world!"

Our hair waves in the breeze.
We are spectators, going no place,
the stationary, the restless.
The cars all purpose and blur, barely people
to us—speed and thrill on wheels.
Jack gets that look in his eyes,
like he often does, sadness or hunger.
I say, "Let's play *Guess where?*"

He smiles and comes back to me—
my best friend for life.
We've stood here so many times
guessing where they're going.
I point at a blue van and shout: "California!"
He points to three in a row: "Memphis!
Las Vegas! New York!" We name everywhere
we can think of, anywhere but across town
to the dentist or to school.

Everyone is in motion but us.
We anchor the bridge
with our need.

DISCONNECTED

When I get home,
Dad's reappeared. I don't say much
while I'm exploring the fridge
for an after-school refuel.

"Quinnie, we're not connecting,"
Dad tells me.

I think: *You're never home.*

I say: "Oh yeah?"

"When I'm home, you shut yourself
up in your bedroom. Gaming."

I think: *I might be doing homework—or writing.*

I say: "I'm doing homework."

"Quinnie, I'm trying here."

I think: *When you *are* home,*
you're on your phone blogging
about your third child:
the Great Outdoors. Or fighting
with Mom.

I say: "Thanks, Dad.
We could hang right now."

"Uh . . . okay"—he pauses—
"I gotta take care of
a couple bills first." Short for:
See you in a couple hours.

"Actually—I was just heading out
to skate. Jack's teaching me
to ollie over stuff. He says
I can get it with a little
more practice."

PARKING LOT

Jack messages:

    At the lot

When I get there,
I don't expect Jade—

and her long legs and long braids
and good mood.

When I see her,
I visualize my friendship
with Jack slipping away.
It's not jealousy;
she's just a better skater,
maybe a better friend.
I stop my brain
from thinking this,
so as not to materialize it.

It'd be easy
not to like Jade—
but she greets me with
"Quinnie!"
and offers a fist bump.
She's just cool like that.

Her mom must've
dropped her off
in our part of town.
Again.

She and Jack are working
on sticking an ollie
over two steps down
to the sidewalk.

I sit on my board,
the board I bought because Jade said
to be a real skater you gotta have this kind.

I study them. I can plain ollie,
and I can kinda ollie while moving,
but I can't ollie over
anything. Not yet. Jack skates
over, pops the nose
of his board up to his
hand, and sits
down. "What's new, Q?"
He can read my face,
always can.

"Same."

He says, "Good talk,"
trying to cheer me up.

I snag some gravel,
toss it. "Dad blames
his distance on *my* gaming.
Not his absence."

"Typical.
Sorry, Quinnie. Hey, I can
teach you." He points
to Jade sticking a
beauty of an ollie.

"Yo, Jack," she yells,
"see that?"

"Destroyed it," Jack calls.

"Come on."
He hops up, grabs
a stick, and puts
it on the pavement.
"Start with this.
It's a rule of three:
Go fast, so the board won't slip.
Look where you want to land.
Then stomp the bolts
and scoop the nose up."

He demonstrates,
makes it look easy-breezy.

Jade skates to us, ollies
up and over the stick
without giving it
a second thought.

"Cool." I nod
and wait until
they're back to the steps
to hoist myself up
off the ground.

Each time I get close,
my board hits the stick.
I attempt it like
forty times.

Jack calls, "Lower your body
and bend your knees to get more
height." Jade agrees.

NAILED IT—NOT!

Lying in the grass under a tree,
we three stare up through the branches.
Jack and Jade, glowing with success.
I'm a sweaty mess.

"You gotta go fast and commit,"
Jade says, assuming
the role of master skate Jedi.

I'm taking mental notes,
not just about skating
but also on how she handles herself.
Jack hangs on her every word.

"Just not feeling it today," I lie.

She shrugs.

"What would you rather
ollie over," Jack asks, "a crocodile pit
or a bottomless pit?"

"Obviously crocs," Jade says,
"a little bite's nothing
to gone for good.
What about," Jade joins in,
"pool of lava or pool of broken glass?"

"Glass," Jack says.
"Lava leaves no room
for mistakes."

"True enough!" Jade says.

All I'm thinking
is maybe a stick
or maybe a curb.

SKATE FOR LIFE?

The feel
of board under feet
isn't cutting it, giving me
the usual boost
and grounding
me to something
other than me.

I prop it
next to my front door,
sink down to sitting
on the porch—
not ready to enter—
and pull a piece
of notebook paper
from my bag.

The pencil feels
kinda just-right
in my hand.
And by that—
I mean I feel
just a little
capable.

THE FIGHT BEFORE

You'd think a driver's license,
college degree,
parenthood, and a real job
would teach you how to fight
about things that matter,
but the evidence points to nope—
at least not in this home.

It's about a shower curtain this time.
Yep—a shower curtain!

Dad presents—or yells—his case:
>*The purple splatter*
>*in the middle reminds me of when*
>*Forrest ran for senior class president*
>*and painted a hundred campaign signs by hand.*

For someone who doesn't shower here,
he sure has a lot to say about the matter.

Mom rebuts:
>*It's a stain.*
>*That's all people see.*
>*Forrest would agree.*
>*Besides, why do YOU care?*
>*You're barely home. And I*
>*feel like redecorating.*

If I made that stain,
this would be a nonissue.
Both parents would insist:
Clean up after yourself.
Use your allowance to replace it.

I walk away,
to Forrest's room.
At his door, I close my eyes
to listen for his feet
keeping beat to his trumpet.
But his feet
and trumpet

are in another state.
So I let myself in,
sit on his comforter,
which smells like cologne,
detergent, and
perfection.

I whisper,
"Quinnie says *Forrest,*
come home."

When I was younger,
I would stand at his bedside,
yank on this very comforter.
Forrest, spotlighted
in the glow of his lamp,
notebooks stacked beside him.
More than once, he was asleep.
so I clicked off the light,
pulled his comforter up
to his chin,
and tucked my big brother in.

This comforter, not so different
from a shower curtain, is comforting.

I whisper,
"Quinnie says *Forrest,*
come home."

Downstairs,
the back door is closing.
And now Mom's bedroom door
is slamming
upstairs.

GAMING WITH JACK

We've grown up gaming.
First it was hide-and-seek,
tag, chase, and whatever.
Then we got consoles.
Adventure, RPGs,
shooters.

"If you could play
only one game for the rest
of your life, what
would it be, Quinnie?"

For a second,
I consider his question,
like it's life or death.

"I don't know—maybe *Cloud Rush*."

"No way! There's no fame
in that game, no scores even.
War Droid all the way," he says.

I wonder if Jade plays *War Droid*—
if I need to check it out,
try to match her top score.

I sigh and change the topic.
"I'm never gonna stick an ollie-over."

"You will. You gotta learn to fall,
to bail out to protect yourself—
run off the board, slide with your knees,
or roll out of the impact.
Once you lose
your fear of falling,
it's a cinch."

Then Jack shoots my man dead.

"Dude!" I yell.

"Like I said, you gotta learn to bail
before you get hurt."

THE NIGHT BEFORE

Pumpkin turns circles
in his fun wheel.
"Chill out, little guy.
My brain's awake too.
I know how you feel."

He looks at me.
Wiggles his cute nose.
"Hello, friend," I say.
"I love you."

I replay their argument in my head,
replay doors closing/slamming,
Mom crying
in her bedroom.
Me standing at her
door, helpless,
listening.

I switch mind channels.
Envision a game with Jade and Jack—
I'm dominating for once,
securing a win against
them—*Victory!*

I switch mind channels again.
Picture the skate park,
Jack in golden light
as he comes off a ramp.
But even as I'm directing this dream,
Jade comes off the ramp
right after him—
in perfect form,
sharing his sunshine.

During and
Immediately After

THE RIGHT BEFORE

Sirens singing
nudging, tricking me.
Am I asleep? Still dreaming?
Is it my dumb alarm beeping?
Or the late-to-school bell sneaking
into my stress
nightmare?

Wait—it's 2 a.m.!

I slump up to my elbow,
jot some random thoughts into my phone
about the whistling wind
and slamming rain.
Maybe tomorrow, I'll try
to turn this
into a poem.

Covers back up & over
this sleepy head.
And it's back to bed!

FALSELY ALARMING

My bedside is buzzing
buzzzz buzzzz buzzzz-ing.
Not a ding message from Jack.
buzzzz buzzzz buzzzz-ing.
Mom and Dad would wake me
if it were important.
buzzzz buzzzz buzzzz-ing
"Shut up!" I grab and toss
my rude phone into
a pile of laundry.

The wind begins to groan.
In a sleep fog, I wonder
Wait—is Dad home?
In bad weather, he's the one
who always steers us,
flashlight in hand,
into the dank basement.

Fact: old houses like mine
have haunted
basements with earthen floors
and cobweb curtains,
unjolly Christmas trees,
a forgotten crib, or moldy bear.
Can't fall asleep NOW—picturing
that bear, listening to
the rain. Weather like this

has always been
a false alarm. Dad says
the city's new storm sirens
are too sensitive.

But there it goes again!

Singing,
singing, singing,
singing me back
to an unpeaceful
half sleep.

NOCTURNAL

Light enough to see
Pumpkin's going places
on his wheel, circulating,
getting around, scritch-
scratching his cedar chips.
Him and the wind stalking
loneliness into the night,
the only ones still wide awake
in this stormy world.

VOLUME-CRANKED

A scream
        in the dark
                belongs to Mom,
filled with fear,
                urgency.
"Quinn, get up!"

Nightgowned figure
in my doorway.

Her words
        don't
                register.

"Up!
      Now!"

Volume cranked
over ten. I jump to my feet,
stumble, recover,
follow her to the top
of the stairs.

Objects start smACKing
                the house.
We don't think
        to turn on the lights.

Hesitate for a sec, listen to the ruckus outside—
strange quality to the air—
as walls of noise
surround us.

      Is it hail? More like rocks.
More than rocks. Bricks?
We sprint
         down
            the stairs,
legs
shaking
unsteady, Mom grabs
my arm and pulls me
            to the basement.
The storm
howls and growls, growing
angrier. Then glass explodes,
shattering our things,
hitting floors. Mom flings open
            the basement door—
                 as the world outside
suddenly quiets,
then comes to a whispering standstill—
a total
eerie
dark
S I L E N C E.

60 SECONDS

That's all it took.
"Maybe it's over?"
Mom whispers,
as if some shady storm guy
is lurking right outside,
coming for us.

We stand side by side.
Adrenaline-wired.

"Where's Dad?" I ask.

"Grandma Jo's.
Left last night."

"Oh," I say.

We stand there
for ten minutes,
or maybe more,
waiting
for the storm
to buck up again.

Just
breathing,
breathing,
breathing.

THE MOMENT IT BECOMES CLEAR

When we move,
I see that glass covers
our floors like party confetti—
but not a party you'd want to attend.
Luckily, Mom put on slippers
before waking me.

"Stay here!"
Her hand feeling for the way,
flipping on lights that don't respond,
maneuvering over things
I can't see.

She brings sneakers
like a poststorm gift.
When we move
together from our spot,
we notice the air—thick
and moist, like the outdoors
has been invited in.
Few windowpanes remain,
and puddles of rain
pool here and there.
Some of our things have shifted
from where they'd been,
from shelves and tables
to the floor.

A bad storm.
A near miss.

Or so we think.

Until
      we open

the front door.

UNREAL—

There is no other word.

Inside our broken home,
we don't know how broken
the outside world is.

Like that old film
The Wizard of Oz,
in the landing-in-Oz scene,
where Dorothy opens
the door of her gray house
to reveal a new world
in multicolor.

Or like *Willy Wonka*
and the Chocolate Factory
when he visits the factory
and everything dazzles
candy-pop colorful.

One of those oldies
parents make you watch
because it "defined" their childhood
and *You Have to See It Too!*

Like that, but not colorful
or happy. Although I guess
you could almost see it as festive,
like someone decorated our yard.

Reality hitting:
     This was MORE than a bad storm!

Still, I think only: *Wow,*
         the yard
            has a bunch of stuff in it.

But with each minute,
our eyes and understanding widen.

"I think it was a tornado," Mom says.

SURREAL

So maybe
there is
another word
or two
to describe
it—

surreal

an eighth-grade vocabulary word,
a synonym of *unreal,* as are
delusive, impalpable,
intangible, hallucinatory,
and my new favorite,
phantasmagoric.

Thanks, Ms. Koval,
for filling my head
with all these
unbelievable
words!

YARDFUL

Dad used to keep our property
mowed and flowered,
trimmed and tidy.

Not as much lately.
But still, the mess is clear,
even with no porch lights
no golden-eyed windows
no streetlights.

I make a mental list
standing on our porch
next to Mom, who's also
openmouthed, taking it in:
fluff-soggy insulation,
shiny-sided metal,
parts of a roof—maybe?
shingles, bricks, and spears
of splintered wood
stabbing into our grass,
a metal porch chair,
with a pillow still on it!
Gutters twisted like licorice.
A parade of random objects—
a shoe, an umbrella, a mailbox.
And trash—so much trash.
As if all the cans barfed up
their contents.

People tumble out of doors,
stumble into their yards
into the after-storm quiet,
dots of bobbing flashlights
and uncertain ambling.

"You guys okay over there?"
college-guy Rashad,
who rents next door,
shouts to us.

"We're okay," Mom replies.
"You?"

"Yeah."

From our yard,
we recognize power lines hanging,
a scrambling of belongings in the road,
foreign objects in other people's yards.
We walk our path to the sidewalk,
stepping over the dark shapes
that invaded our space.
"Be careful," Mom cautions.
We peer down the road.
"What's that?"

It looks like—but can't be—
the church's steeple squatting
in the middle of the road.
And the historic firehouse
at the end of the block—
what's wrong with it?
The roof. It's gone.
Oh my gosh!
Oh my gosh!
Oh my gosh!

We don't get far, since
power lines crisscross and
snake the street
where they don't belong.
In passing, someone tells us
to listen for gas leaks.

Three doors down,
a tall house is opened up,
now a one-story, a portion
of the second floor ripped off.
Other parts of it collapsed.
Its couple huddles in their front yard,
her clutching a dog, him a guitar.
"Who are they?" I whisper to Mom.

"You know, Whatserface
and her husband."

We keep walking,
saying to each other
maybe that's where
the damage stops,
drawing an imaginary
line, to control all
our out-of-control
feelings.

"At least we're okay," Mom says.
"A few roofs. The steeple—
all this can be fixed,
picked up tomorrow
when the power
is restored."

And when the sun turns on
its big overhead light.

AFTER SILENCE—NOISE

Making our way back home,
Mom's phone starts dinging
in her bathrobe pocket:
Grandma Jo. Then a colleague
of Mom's "checking in."
Ambulances and police cars
begin to whine in the distance.
Somewhere, security alarms
belonging to houses or
businesses are blaring.
We hear people shouting.

THANKFUL

"We're okay.
At least we're okay,"
Mom says again and again,

her breath coming in gasps,
her arm around me. I try
to see her face in the dark.
"It could've been so much worse."

Little do we know,
it *was* so much worse
for so many
around us.

ENCOUNTER WITH A DRUNK GIRL

She trips and stumbles by,
coming from a nearby bar,
muttering words to us
and anyone else:
"I gotta find
my boyfriend."
Mom tries to warn
her. "You shouldn't
go that way. You'll step
on a power line or glass."
But she stumbles on,
shoves past Mom.
"I gotta find
my boyfriend,"
she mumbles again.

AND STRANGER STILL

A car's headlights
pierce the dark road
in front of our house.
A car trying to drive
over rubble, like it's
any other day;
its wheels crunch and
hit metal, until it is
forced to stop.
Then, as if
strange sights are in,
just the latest trend,
around the corner
comes Dad—on a bike.
A bike! He leaps off,
drops it at the edge
of our yard, and runs to us.
"I had to park my car"—
he catches his breath—
"a few blocks away, couldn't
get through. Trees down
everywhere. Found this bike.
Are you okay?"
"Why didn't you call?" Mom says.
"I was too busy
trying to get to you."
He pulls her to him

and hugs us both.
"I'm sorry I wasn't here."

In the dark,
I feel Mom relax,
give in to the hug.

AMBULANCE STORY

It cries in the distance,
trying to make its way through.
We play the guessing game
where it's heading,
until it parks at the corner
and two medics pop out
and unload a stretcher.
Our eyes track their path
to a nearby house, the Wests'.
With Dad, we walk over,
ask, "Can we help?"
When they ease Mrs. West out
and onto the stretcher, a slow
trickle of blood in her white hair,
we make a volunteer line
like a bucket brigade
to haul bricks from the sidewalk
so they can wheel her
to the ambulance—
to safety.

UNDER ONE ROOF—TOGETHER

We won't be able to do much
until morning—and some of us need
to sleep. Tornado or not—I'm a teenager.
I can catch Zs on my desk.
Snooze on the bus during rush hour.
On a park bench in the sunshine.
In the back of Mom's car.
Um—pretty much anywhere:
once I fell asleep in a tree.

Mom shakes debris
from a blanket and covers me.
I float off into turbulent dreams,
their voices blending in a nearby room,
a song of a family reunited, a dad
come home, under one roof again,
a roof mostly in one piece, a shelter over
our heads in the candlelit dark.

WHILE I SLEEP

Dad goes back out,
helps neighbors until 6 a.m.,
sees more ambulances arrive,
live wires located, falling dangers
secured, a few fires averted.

I sleep through it all, hunkered
down on a dry futon in a room
with the windows still intact.

WHEN SUDDENLY YOU REMEMBER YOUR PET

It takes a few blinks
to recall the night,
to wipe sleep from my eyes
and tell truth from nightmare.
From this lying-down angle,
the outdoors looks blue-sky beautiful.
The sun strikes me—
and I bolt upright.

What kind of person forgets their pet?

I stand, and take in several things—
the windowpanes scratched and cracked and caked with dust

AND

the buzz that will become the soundtrack of my neighborhood.

I leap up, stumble over books,
stacked around me like a fort,
some left open to dry.

Did Mom do that while I slept?

In the kitchen, she stands
staring at the cold coffeemaker.

"Where's Dad?"
I don't wait for her reply
as I head to my room.

"Hardware store," she calls after me,
"trying to get plywood before it's all gone."

Our house
looks like a giant
has given it a good shake,
the way you would
a game of Boggle:
cabinets opened,
drawers askew,
things slipped or spilled.

"The stairs are blocked
with pictures that fell.
I haven't started on that yet,"
Mom shouts.

"I have to get up there—Pumpkin!"
I pull on sneakers
and go.

School pictures shattered,
Forrest's prize essay torn,
his graduation picture smashed,
parts of the frame on the stairs.
I step over him,
fragments of glass
surrounding his face.

THE UPSTAIRS

I'm not prepared
for what I find (or don't find):
Pumpkin's cage on the floor, the door bent open.
The shower curtain from last night's fight
pulled down and used to mop up water
from around my window and my desk.
Books scattered and sopping, propped
like I was reading, technology trashed, branches
and bark everywhere, leaves stuck like stickers
to my things, the dresser wiped clean, patchy wet carpet,
shingles on my blanket where I'd been sleeping,
and a muck stew coating it all.

"Mom!" I call, searching the wood shavings
and Pumpkin's wheel. Mom's somewhere
in the house taking pictures and doesn't answer.
"Pumpkin's gone!" I yell, scanning the floor
around the cage, puzzle pieces of glass
on every surface.

I picture his tiny paws cut and bleeding.

I tap his food bowl, a sound he likes.
But he doesn't come scurrying
out from under anything. I get down
on my stomach, peer into Pumpkin-
sized hiding places. I glance at the
open window, the tree branch
entering my room,
like a bridge into the wild.
He could be anywhere.
Anywhere!

THE DARK HAS A WAY OF DOWNPLAYING

Sunlight deals it straight
when we move outside—
neighbors stand,
hands in pockets, stand
in yards, helpless, stand
on sidewalks, in the street,
staring, wordless, standing
like old friends, people we'd never
talked to, even though our houses
are feet apart, like Rashad.
My family always too busy—
up & dressed & off to work
or school, straight into the car,

Mom looking the other way
or at a phone, to avoid the waves,
the others' eyes. No time
for small talk, no space
on the old hard drive.

ON REALLY SEEING MY HOUSE, I WRITE THIS ODE IN MY HEAD

More than an address.
Holder of my childhood,
our once-upon-a-time happiness,
a memory box of keepsakes,
place where I play,
eat, grow, sleep and wake—
shaken and broken,
in need of repair.

IN SHOCK AND TAKING STOCK

of what the tornado took
as it tore a path through us.
A list that will triple in time.
Not only *stuff*
but abstract nouns too.

Ms. Koval taught us
that nouns are things
that can be abstract or concrete:
security, comfort, and *belonging.*
And *home.*
(Maybe if more homes were concrete
they wouldn't be damaged so easily.)

Mom hands me a box
for salvaging.
My computer has ponds
of water on top.
The keyboard dangles
by its cord. My headphones
are heaped with odds and ends
on the floor. A branch
from the dogwood lies
across my desk. If I'd
been there, I'd be treed.

I search for my phone, which
had been buzzing, trying
to warn me. Now missing.
My clothes—one thing I don't
care about—seem to be
perfectly fine, hanging
in my closet. The posters
peel back in the damp.

It seems my skateboard,
which I'd left on the porch,

rolled away. Nothing that was mine
yesterday is mine today.

DISCOVERY

How were we not hurt?
Anything tall,
like telephone poles,
got toppled,
and so many of the giant old trees
in the neighborhood.

We hear *Three people lost their lives.*

I circle our house
and make a discovery.
My dogwood—its buds
still waiting to bloom,
the notched-petal flowers
that signal summer is coming,
that I've survived another year
of school—is totally uprooted
and lying on its side.

I look up to my bedroom window,
and back down at the tree
that was as old as me. I swallow
a sob that begins somewhere
deep in my chest.

OUR HOUSE AMONG THE OTHERS

"We were lucky," Mom says calmly,
like she's ready for life and work to resume.
She and Dad walk the yard side by side, inspecting,
making a second call to the insurance guy, as I trail behind
sifting through tufts of grass for Pumpkin.
Our list of damage grows, with Mom's car windows
smashed and our shed squashed.

Some houses near ours still have plants
and deck furniture unstirred, yet others' porches
were swiped clear off.

"Look!" Dad calls from our backyard.
A tree house that used to be in one neighbor's backyard
now lodged in the backyard of another.
Maybe the kids were like *Look what the tornado brought us!*
It's almost funny.
If we could laugh.

THE WALK

As a trio,
we walk like tourists
in a new land, sad sightseers,
bonded by what we witness—
the path of the tornado so obvious
as it cut new vantages of the downtown.

We can see clear through to the park.
All eyeballs, we are separate from what we see
but a part of it too. "No one watches live TV,"
Dad mumbles, trying to comprehend
how there were no clear warnings. The flagpole
at the firehouse now at an angle, dangling its flag
like it lowered itself to half-staff. We trek
for blocks and blocks, blue tarps covering
houses as far as you can see. I imagine houses shivering
and in shock beneath them. We pass not one,
but three news crews—the irony of others
elsewhere seeing all this on TV, while we cannot
begin to grasp the magnitude, without electricity.
"All I'd heard was a storm that 'might produce tornados,'
and 'threat level three.'" Dad still trying to solve
the unsolvable equation of nature.
Mom walks closer to him than usual,
their hands almost touching—or maybe
I imagine that. "Who could predict *this*?" she says.
It's on this walk that one of my feet
begins to pinch with each step,
like glass or something has embedded
itself into my sole.

At some point, when we can't see anymore,
we pass Ivy Manor and see a dog going bonkers
in the backyard, jumping up over and over again,
so only its head appears above the fence.
The three of us stop for a bit of comic relief.

Dad asks, "Did this place get hit?"

"No, it's been run-down for a while," Mom tells him.

SOMEONE SAYS, "EF4 ON A SCALE OF 1 TO 5"

Ms. Koval taught us recently
that *personifying* is a way of dressing
a thing up in human clothes
to help us understand or see it better.
I wonder if we will ever understand
why the tornado—which they've given
a number now—chose us.

Does a rating
help adults pretend
they can forecast and protect
from forces bigger than themselves?
Like naming a hurricane, Anne or Julian,
makes it more forgiving,
as if you could reason with it—
"Please don't pick my home."

I think the cousin to the hurricane
is the tornado, who crashes your event,
throws a party at your house, ransacks,
and vanishes before catching any heat
for dropping by.

UN-HOUSED

Dad tosses utility gloves
to me. Mom uncharacteristically
walks over to chat up a neighbor,
then settles not too far from us,
on the porch to wash the outdoors
off indoors stuff. We are
a united family front.

Dad and I sort piles, remove wreckage.
He hauls plywood up to the roof
in the bright afternoon sun.
I daydream he's fixing
Every.
Thing.
                Isn't that what dads do?

I steady his ladder.
He doesn't let me come up.
If Forrest were here, he'd be up there
working with Dad, laughing, joking,
helping to make the world solid again.

I replay five of Forrest's words
that always catch and stick in my mind:
"They never fought before you!"

He was mad when he said it,
but soon after, they split up for twenty-eight days.

That's pretty much a month,
though it felt like a year.

They'd been fighting about my trash grades,
which, come to think of it, were mostly
because I didn't turn work in.
I mean, it worked, didn't it?
I got their attention.

Mom wanted to hire a tutor.
"Let her be," Dad had argued.
"Failure is the best way to learn."
I know he didn't mean it, but that word
also stuck, like a nail through wood.
Hello! My name is Failure.
Like a label on my forehead.
Like the letter *F*.

Last year, when letter
after letter crammed our mailbox—
scholarships and acceptances—and I
was still getting Cs and Ds and sometimes a B,
I realized Forrest would always be
something I could never be.

Dad curses from the roof,
so I climb up to the top rung.
"I can pass you nails," I offer.
He bends over jagged holes,
hammering and patching, so the next
rain won't enter uninvited.

REPAIR OR STATE OF DISREPAIR?

When Mom finally tunes in
to us and notices the piles
we've made of what to trash
and what to keep, she inserts herself:
"Just throw it all away.
And don't bother recycling."

I think of all our hard work
and quick-change the subject
so Dad won't disagree.
"What about power?" I ask.
He thinks we can get by another night
in the dark, on the futon and couch.
Mom suggests a hotel.
Under his breath he mutters,
"One room or two?"

"Like we're on vacation," I say,
looking from one to the other—
then leave to give them
space to discuss.

I'm sore, my hands hurt,
but I walk and walk, like I can't get enough.
People are everywhere. I pass car after car
with windows smashed, and one overturned.
I can't help but stare at people's homes.
In one, a toilet and shower are exposed

on a second floor. I look away,
embarrassed. Houses spill themselves into yards,
cough their curtains out their windows
as if they've grown tired of their people:
"And take all your stuff too!"
Photos from more than one waterlogged album
are scattered like fall leaves in the grass.
In the Wests' yard, I find a wedding photo
displayed in cracked glass and broken frame.
I walk it to their porch and place it on a chair.
Everyone's secrets are on display—
their fences have come down.
In another house, I spy a closetful
of hangers. In yet another, I see
a blanketed bed and overhear a cluster
of people saying the woman
rolled left. If she had rolled right,
she would've rolled out of bed
and out of the house. I'm awed
at the small decisions and reactions
with the power to change lives.

TAKING GREATER STOCK

The first night after,
in the strange poststorm dusk,
Mom, Dad, and I regroup on our front porch,
since there's more light outside than inside,

sharing what we've heard and seen.
The number of buildings damaged,
churches, schools, businesses, and what they know
about the three people who lost their lives.
"I could've lost you two," Dad says,
and looks away to hide his face.
I look at Mom for her reaction,
which she keeps to herself.

People pass by on the sidewalk and call
out to us, *Do you need anything?*
Can we help you? They offer us wet wipes,
gloves, and trash bags. It hasn't sunk in—
how we're victims too. And I don't know yet
what we need.

UNPLUGGED

It hits me:
"I have to *type* my poetry project
and I have no computer. No phone.
The power has to come back on!"

"You'll manage for a few days," Mom says.
"You'll survive," Dad says.

>   Whiplashed
>   by their unity—

but not wanting to jinx it,
just needing
to think on it—
I head to the park,
in the last embers of light,
and make out Jack and Jade
packing up, leaving side by side,
and laughing. I want to ask them,
What's so funny?

"I texted you, Quinnie," Jack tells me.

I hold up my empty hand.
"No phone. It's missing."

"Sorry about your house.
Come hang tomorrow. No school again!
We're skating."

"Yeah, no board either."

"That's tragic," Jade says.
"I have an old one
you can borrow."

But I don't want Jade's.
Besides, another day out of school
is for those of us who are unlucky
and recuperating.

OLD-SCHOOL

On one of Dad's trips
back and forth to Grandma Jo's the next day,
she sends a spiral notebook with him—
"For Quinnie to capture her thoughts.
Not everyone lives through a tornado."
Dad also brings back home
some of his clothes.

My hands are twitchy,
after one night of no gaming.
I wonder if Jack's already found new opponents
to replace me. Suddenly time
feels slo-mo and I have nothing to do
except write.

CALL FROM FORREST

"The neighborhood
made the news.
I was worried
about you guys."

He wants to know
how his room is.
It was miraculously
spared. "Good," he says,

"though most of my stuff is
here, safe with me."
Including his
big personality.

At least he thinks
to ask about Pumpkin
and tell me he's sorry.

"Dad's back," I say.
He waits. Then says, "Ohh-kay,"
and adds, "Tread lightly.
Don't get in their way, Quinnie."

"What do you mean?"

"Just don't stress them out.
They have enough
to worry about."

I hang up Mom's phone.

THINGS YOU TAKE FOR GRANTED UNTIL THEY'RE GONE

Cold food. Ice cubes.
A light that comes on
when you walk in a room

and flip a switch. Air-conditioning.
Windows, keeping bugs and moths out.
Checking your phone for a song,
the date, a restaurant's menu.
Asking your phone the time and weather.
The privacy of shutting your door.
Messaging friends.
Being in touch.

ODE TO THE TREES

I didn't really see
trees before the tornado.
I climbed them,
swung from them,
shaded under them.
There was the dogwood,
my own personal tree,
but others were just background,
like clouds and sky,
skyscrapers and bridges.
Now I notice them,
their absence,
where they used to be,
used to canopy streets.
Or as landmarks
for navigating—
Turn by the big tree in the park!

Meet you at the magnolia.
Now everything is bright,
open, light that used to be filtered
through branches and leaves—
now glares. Parts of them remain
jagged and broken, things
strung up like decoration—
roofing, insulation, wires, trash.
Piles of wood accumulating
on every block. If I don't
remember the trees in a poem,
I may not remember them
at all. And paper! Thanks
for all this paper, trees!

TYPING VS. WRITING

No games
or websites
or distractions
convincing me to look
or shop or play
or watch.

Just thoughts from my head
to my hand—
pencil tip
to
paper.

The relationship
is so simple:
just like that
I bring to life
the tornado . . .

TORNADO

My temper hits lightning-quick

                                    in a flash.
You can try to read the signs, the foreshadowing.

                    I'm ramping up, brewing, losing it
            people warn each other

                        when they see me stewing,
see me coming. Experts track me, but I'll level with you: I'm out
of control.

                        I do what I do.

        Houses, barns, swing sets, cars—these are my playthings
                                        I pick
                            one up, catapult
                            it,

                    snatch another, break it, smash
            it, snap it,
snag a person from a couch and flop them like a doll
I spin, howl, punch, roar,

                toss anything in my way,
throw a tantrum for blocks or miles across towns and states
Un-

        predict-

                able
        Casting what I want
        to the ground
                Un-

                        for-

                            giving
Call me a bully—see if I care

I pick on some,
leave others be.
Uproot people and trees
De-
stroy-
ing
You'll know
    where I've been
        Left my mark
            'cause I'm hurt&anger&pain
                swirled into
                one
        Can't hide from me
                unless I choose
                you're not worth my time
                I'll kick and bruise you for fun,
                that's who
                        I am
Un-
      do-
            ing
all the work people have done
Twisting.
Turning.
Sweeping.
Churning.
Plucking.
Taking.
Taking.
Taking.

WILDLIFE

I imagine Pumpkin
on the go, making
a run, busted free—
loose in the wild world.
Three inches of chubby fuzz-body, fending
for himself, averting danger—or maybe,
on a grand adventure.

Can't help but picture
a hungry hawk
eyeing his not-so-slender figure,
a feline making a beeline to munch him.
So much for being
a decent caretaker of small animals!
Scratch that off
my potential expertise list.

Poststorm, even deer
have wandered from
the depths of City Park
into the streets and yards,
a disoriented dash and flash of white tail,
then back to the woods,
to their comfort zone.

One neighbor mentions the rats
he's counted, scurrying

from demolished structures
and out from under
an overturned dumpster.

Which is not all that different
from the people
looking lost and aimless,
a kitchen pot in one hand
a shovel or broom
in the other.

But the storm shuffled more than
wildlife and people's stuff;
it brought Dad
out of the country,
back home to us.

LEGO GIRL

Nature rearranged
my bedroom, but we don't
share a vision, so I attempt
to return things to where they belong.
"Don't bother." Dad leans in my doorway.
"We need to wait until
the big stuff is deemed fixable."

Is the "big stuff" the roof,
the windows, maybe me—
or Mom and Dad's marriage?

I drop a ruined poster to the floor
and head to the porch,
where I collapse and let sweat
drip off my neck. That's when I spy
the Lego girl planted
in the flower bed.

She must've skated
off my desk in the storm.
Finding her now might be a sign.
Some things will get back
to normal soon.

DROP-BY

Humiliating to be
standing in your front yard
in yesterday's clothing, stained
and stinky, holding most everything
you own in a trash bag, when your
friends saunter up. Jack and Jade
carry their boards, due to the torn-up road.
Mom nods. "Take a break, Quinn."

I drop the bag and tag along
to the park, each step
a small pinch in my foot
I still forgot to check.
"When I jumped out of bed

that night, I think I stepped in glass,"
I tell them.

Jade wrinkles her nose
and hops on her board.
They skate to a curb.
Jade jumps it. Jack jumps it.
"Quinnie," Jack offers, "you wanna take
a turn on my board?"

"I'm good."

They skate back to where I stand.
"You know, my mom and I
made it to the basement entrance
right as it all stopped."

They are not rude.
They listen. They nod.

"So weird," Jade responds.
"It barely rained at my house."

"I slept through it," Jack agrees.

O TO BE WILD

I sit back and marvel at Jack—
growing more and more fearless on his board,
never considering the break or bruise.
Giving it all he's got, one hundred percent.
Clearly, he's taking notes
from Jade.

"Jack—what are we thinking
for your birthday?
Isn't it coming up?" Jade asks.

Jack will tell her, "Nothing."
Every year, he says
his dad might come home
to take him somewhere.
Usually, his dad
doesn't show.

"How 'bout Eastside skate park?"
Jade says between tricks.
"We could go there, then pizza?"

"He's not big on birthdays," I tell
Jade, giving Jack a knowing look.
"Right—your dad?"

"Screw him," Jack says.

"I thought you said—"

"Yeah, screw him," Jade chants.

I think about my wrecked
computer, my absence
from our online meetup.
It's only been like a day and a half—
and he's already sounding
more like Jade.

WITHOUT A BOARD, I USE MY FEET TO WALK HOME

From a block away,
I glimpse them—promise myself
not to feel anything, especially hope.
Among the destruction, they sit
on the porch, knees touching, his arm drapes
her shoulders, she leans her head on him.
They see me approaching
and don't move from their position.
With each step, I let the pinch
in my foot remind me how hurt hides.
And at the exact same time
Dad says, "Hey, Quinnie!"
Mom says,
"Hello, Quinn!"

SOME OF US MOVE OUT

On the third day, which feels like eons,
Mom and I pack up to leave. There's not a lot
worth taking. We trash the last of our food
from the fridge. My right hand hangs loose
at my side, my left clutches a garbage bag.
I sift through my other things with my foot.
Boy—a storm knows how to clean house.
My skateboard is still missing. I stand there
imagining some other kid coasting on it, and
I'm not sure how much I've actually missed it.

Dad suggests we stay at Grandma's.
Mom says she won't leave the city,
she needs to be nearby for work.
A friend of hers found a couple rooms
for us, right here in the neighborhood.
By dusk, we're done packing the car.

Dad plans to rough it, camp out, make do,
and live in our house while he fixes it.

NOT THIS PLACE!

Even in the dark,
I know the house.

"Not

     THIS

          place!"

I protest as we pull up.
It looms before us
all dank, doom, and neglect.

My eyes bug out.
"You know who lives here, right?"

Mom pulls Grandma's borrowed car
into the overgrown drive.
Ivy hangs in places where ivy shouldn't,
barely any house peeks out—
and what shows is peeling paint
and wooden decay.

Mom parks, folds her hands in her lap.
"We don't have much choice.
Plus, it's close to my work. Our home.
And Dad. Besides, it's free."

I sit, refusing to budge,
to acknowledge her list of reasons.

"I thought you'd like it.
It's right across from the park."
Mom points back toward City Park.

"Why not a hotel?
And how do you know
this creepy old dude?"

"I don't. Julia from work,
he's her dad."

"People avoid this place.
At Halloween, it's the one you egg
or roll. And I heard he had something
to do with that missing girl—
and that he poisons dogs."

"Rumors—and cruel!" Mom
shakes her head. "Have you seen
what someone did
to the historic marker out front?"

I don't mention
that Jack was the one
who "redesigned"
the sign in the yard of the house—
        from *Ivy Manor*
to *Ivy Man*.

WITH THE WORMS

Mom whips candles and a flashlight
from her bag. "Our new normal!"

"You didn't tell me
the power's out here too!"

"He's getting a generator
up and running tomorrow."

We locate a key in an envelope
taped to the door of the apartment.

Did I mention it's the basement?

Underground, like with the worms.

It's two bedrooms, one bathroom,
a kitchen-den combo, with high
rectangular windows at ground level.
So all I'll see is the prowler's feet
before I meet my death—
and join those worms.

Darker than dark when we enter.
Smells like old people and Lysol.
Mom leads with the flashlight
and bravado. Shadows of furniture
bump into me. Mom takes one
bedroom; gifts me the other.
When I light my candle, I realize
the walls of my room are covered
in mysterious paintings.

"Mom!" I yell, pointing:
"Weird Old Man's been here!"

"Quinn—you can't call him that.
Call him Mr. Jones." She hands me a blanket
and sheets. "Here, catch up on sleep."

I sit wrapped in the blanket,
trying to write in the flickering light.
Jack will freak
when he hears about this.

        When I wake, sunshine
squeezes through the windows,
reveals the wall painting to be
a meadow scene with a castle and village in the distance.
It's actually really good. I scan the room
and out into the rest of the apartment—
hardwood floors, mismatched
whimsical furniture, a bit dusty
but less than sinister.

I stand and stretch,
dump my garbage bags
onto the bed, and head
out to explore the backyard,
which is an acre or more of trees and rosebushes—
all fenced in. I sit at a picnic table
beside a pair of Adirondack chairs
and a fire pit. Mom comes out,

sits beside me, surveys the place:
"Just needs a little love."

Speaking of—
"So . . . Dad's staying
at our house?"

She takes a long time to answer,
and in the meantime,
props my foot on her lap.
She examines my foot,
says the glass should work its way out
on its own.

"He doesn't mind the mess—
says he can work on it better from there."

She says nothing else about him.
Or about them.

The birds serenade us
in the obvious absence of her words.

After a few minutes, the back
door creaks. Mom and I swing our heads that way
to spy a thin white hand poke out
                        and hold the door open just a crack
                                        as a demon-being
                    explodes out,
                                bounds down the stairs

directly at us.
        I bolt from sitting
right as the thing clobbers me.

MEETING THE WEIRD OLD MAN

Pretty sure I scream like an infant—
until I realize the greeting
is licks and wags and doggy-thrill
to meet me. In my defense,
I have a history with dogs.
Mom hops up and gently leads
it to her, pets it lovingly.

"Frederick!" We both startle
at the gruff voice. "He doesn't meet
new people much." The old man
whistles. "Frederick" bounds
toward him, the weird old man,
at the top of the stairs.

He is hunched slightly, white hair,
white beard, wrinkled and frowning.
He bends over with a lot of trouble
to grab the black dog's collar.

"Thanks, Mr. Jones, for letting
us stay at Ivy Manor," Mom calls.

"It's my daughter's doing.
Up to me, it would be empty."

"Well, thank you. It means a lot."

The old man nods.

"Your dog and I have a bond," Mom adds
in the awkward pause.

"He likes everyone," he snorts.
"Grandson babies him, made him
worthless as a guard dog."

He frowns at me.
"He'll eat anything,
so keep your snacks up.
He's not discriminating,"
he mutters before
closing the door.

MY HISTORY WITH DOGS

"At least Weird Old Man's dog
is friendly," Mom says.

I shake my head
at her attempt
to bond.

"At least it's two separate apartments," I add.

"Julia did mention the dog has a doggie door.
He comes downstairs sometimes."

Great!

I scrunch my eyebrows and nose.
Ever since the biting incident
at City Park, five years ago,
when Mom tried to "rescue" a stray dog
and immediately it bit my arm,
I prefer furry creatures
the size of Pumpkin.

Pumpkin.

Frederick doesn't seem
      like he'd bite—
           but I'm not so sure
              about Mr. Jones.

ASSISTANT

I head over to our house
to act as Dad's assistant,
fetching wood glue,
a screwdriver, caulk, hammer—

whatever he needs. When I
get in the way, I back off.
As his assistant, I keep
our projects organized,
steady the ladder, bring him
a bottle of water, assist in
the cleanup afterward,
and keep my hopes to myself.
But when he takes a break,
I say, "It's cool how you're living
at home again." He nods,
stays silent on the subject.

HUNTING FOR PUMPKIN

Click, click, click—
I make the clicking sound
Pumpkin responds to
as I walk and poke around.

Check a bucket tipped over
beside the porch.
No Pumpkin.

I search the monkey grass.
No luck. *Click, click, click.* I comb through shrubs.
Peek in the smushed
shed. *Click, click, click.*

I go back inside and create

a Sharpie-marker flyer
with a description of Pumpkin—
and Mom's number—
and then tack it
to the closest standing
telephone pole.

THE BEAST

The next morning,
I hear him before I see him—
Frederick bursts into
our basement apartment.

"I'll keep him out of your hair,"
Mom calls from the kitchen-den.
"Hello, Frederick!
You need some loving, huh?
Good boy!"

Then I hear her brief, stiff
one-sided conversation.
On the phone
with Dad.

I wander out, rubbing my eyes
and wondering where they stand,
to find Mom and the dog-beast
snuggled up
on the couch.

"He stinks," I say flatly.

This house!

Plus

A dog!!

Minus me.

"I'm heading out."

HANGING WITH PIGEONS IN THE PARK

Don't tell anyone,
but I talk to pigeons.
It's not too different
from talking to a hamster, right?
Feathery instead of furry.
I tell this one strutting up
beside my bench,
"They split up once
because of me.
But right now, they're a little
better. I think." The iridescent ones
listen the best; we have a bond.
Or maybe they're seeking
bread from my hands.

COMMUNITY COOKOUT

Everyone grills up the meats
thawing from their powerless freezers.
Neighbors haul their grills
to the firehouse and into streets.
The air fills with the smoky yum
of burgers, hot dogs, chicken,
and even steaks. Almost every restaurant
in town has jumped in to donate food.
Folding tables hold bags of chips, doughnuts,
cakes, subs, pasta, casseroles, apples
and oranges, cookies—you name it.
Coolers overflow with icy drinks—
it's free all day every day!
And now the food trucks are getting
on board. Kind people take shifts feeding us.

"What do you want, hon?" a smiling woman
asks, then places two pieces of fried chicken
on my full paper plate. People sit on the grass,
the curb, the street—swapping tornado tales,
looking each other in the eyes,
listening—like time has slowed down.
I see a woman hug another.
I see a man crying.
Mom forgot to bring her phone
and is actually chatting.

I spot Jade and Jack walking past
the community grill, eyes bulging
at the glorious spread.
Who can blame them?

"Check out this buffet!" Jade sees me.
"Glad my mom dropped me
off in *your* neighborhood today!"

They help themselves to overflowing plates—
and then head off, leaving Mom and me
so they can go skate.

"TORNA-CATION"

News spreads social-media quick
when school cancels another two days—
due to power outages and widespread damage.
Jack coined our time off
a "torna-cation."

I guess it affected more
than I thought, but it's hard to know
the extent when you're living in it.
Literally "in the dark."

Ms. Koval was going to teach
us to write a found poem this week.

Seems I "found" some time
to catch up on my project poems.

MEETING

Back at Ivy Manor,
I sit outside, hoping
the dog doesn't hear me
and writing—trying to figure out
what bugged me about
Jade and Jack eating
that food and leaving so quickly.
When the back door opens a crack,
I prepare myself. But out steps a boy,
about my age or older in mismatched
clothes like he reached in his dresser
and grabbed items, eyes closed.

Does he work for the Weird Old Man?

I look away while he totes a large plant
to the patio, blocking his view of me.
Whistling and going about his business,
he begins to water it.

When he's done
with the hose and the plant,
he finally notices me. Walks over

and sits in the Adirondack beside me.
I cut my eyes his way.

"Hi, I'm Ian.
I guess you're staying
in my grandpa's apartment?" he asks
with curious eyes and a smile that quirks up
on one side.

"Uh yeah, Quinn or Quinnie,
our house was damaged."

He flops his hair from his face
with a shake of his head. "Sorry to hear that,
Quinn or Quinnie. What are you writing?"
He nods at my spiral.

I stuff it under my legs,
accustomed to Jack, who would crack
a joke about now.
"Oh . . . um . . . nothing."

"Sometimes I write
about nothing too."

Now he's making fun of me.
This I get. I smirk.

"Sometimes you have
to write about nothing
to get to the something,"
he adds.

What's he going on about?
Sounding like Ms. Koval.

Right then, the beast bursts out
and clobbers Ian, luckily,
instead of me.

"Freddie!" He rubs the dog
and the dog whimpers and whines,
can't get enough of him.

Then he tells me, matter-of-factly,
"Did you know petting an animal
releases endorphins for both you and
the animal?"

Pumpkin crosses my mind.

I raise my eyebrows,
suspicious of Weird Old Man's family,
this dude quoting
like a self-help article.

I pull up my hands
so "Freddie" can't reach them.
He scrounges around below me,
scarfing up crumbs or bugs
and licking the ground.

LACK OF AFFECTION

Mom and Dad arrive
with more of our stuff—
disagreeing on how to unload it.
Surprisingly, they keep it
civil—but not quite
the picture of love.

They don't see us sitting there,
and I'm not a fan of public displays
of the lack of affection, so I tell
Ian, "Gotta go," and hit the road.
I can feel him watching
me walk up the drive.
I cross the street and pass
City Park, then keep walking.

Lately, without my board,
I walk just to walk sometimes,
just to think and breathe in peace.
When I observe an old woman

standing in her yard in cowboy boots
and a bathrobe, hair disheveled,
I can't help but stop and stare
as she shakes a box of kitty food,
looking like she's "nutso,"
as Jack might say.

Her face brightens when she sees me,
like she thinks I'm someone else,
someone who can help.
Before I make a break to escape,
she says, "Come here!"

Not sure what I've gotten into,
not sure how *I* can help this old lady,
not sure of anything these days,
so I comply.

"I'm looking for my cat," she says.
"Peevie, as in a pet peeve."

I laugh out loud,
but she doesn't smile.

"Come on, now!" she says.

I start to scan her place,
since I don't know what else to do.
I notice a tree leaning on her house,

and her fence has fallen onto her garden.
Doesn't she have any grown-up
children who can come help?

Why me?

Like her, I start calling for Peevie too,
and imagine what Jack would say about me.
I walk around her property,
searching the bushes and shed.
I check around the fallen tree,
hoping not to find him there—

                  but then I spy a furry guy
peeping from a gap in the door
to the house's cellar.

"I think I see him," I yell,
surprised to be excited. "Is he golden?"

She comes around the house
with open arms—and
smeared tears
on her face.

The cat darts toward her,
rubs against her leg, purring
motor-loud.

The old lady scoops him up
and smiles at me.

"He's all I've got," she says.

Something in my heart flutters.

When she puts the cat down,
he runs to me and rubs
against my leg
           like he's also thanking me.

SPECTATORS

On the walk back to Ivy, I realize
most of the cars cruising the streets are spectators,
not neighbors navigating the streets to their homes.
The gawkers take pictures, lean far out their windows.
Someone even points at me. And I swear I see a kid
take a selfie with a smashed house
in the background.

EVERYONE ELSE'S PETS

Freddie greets me
like a long-lost friend,
in the backyard of Ivy Man.

He sniffs my legs
up and down. Seems
like everyone else's pets
are drawn to me.
Just not my own.
Ian is gone,
so I plop down,
alone.

"You know what I don't like
about you?" I ask Freddie.

He tilts his head,
follows me to my chair.

"You're a follower.
And you stink."

At that, he rolls over
onto his back
and looks up at me.

"Oh all right!" I pat
his tummy once
with my foot
and he rolls around
as if it's the best
feeling
ever.

THE MASSES DESCEND

By six days out, community organizations
and church groups unload from vans
with take-charge attitudes and purpose in their eyes.
They pour in from across the state, bringing crews
sporting matching T-shirts advertising their group.
Some of their slogans remind Tennessee
"We're the Volunteer State." It's like a festival
or street party, but with destruction. I walk around
staring at these people, who are helping just because
it makes them feel good. They showed up,
asking for nothing and with nothing,
other than some tools and their own hands.

Food stations spread from the firehouse
to every other block, and cases of water are deposited
on every street corner. People walk the streets
calling to families in their front yards and offering to help.
Do you need anything? What can we do?
A roving group of "musicians for a cause" sets up
at City Park, and people gather. The music stirs me,
and I get this weird urge to do something,
other than being a spectator.

ICE CREAM CREW

When Jack skates by,
I wave him down.
We get ice creams and funnel cakes
and settle under a tree.
I wait for him to ask
for an update on my house.

"I can't believe all this stuff is free."
He snaps a pic on his phone
of the food trucks
and posts it.

He shows me his phone.
Jade has already liked his post.

"Come hang, Quinnie," Jack pleads.
"Jade's waiting for us.
She's going to teach me
to do a kick turn on a ramp."

"Sounds fun," I say slowly,
scanning the volunteers
and their positive energy,
thinking about how finding Peevie
made me feel helpful,
like I could actually do something—
like how I've started to feel
putting words on paper.

"I still haven't mastered an ollie-over,
and I don't have my board.
I can't keep up with you two."
I don't tell him it's like we're living
in two different worlds.

"An ollie-over is nothing.
We can take turns on my board!"

"Well," I start,
"I . . . I think I might try
to volunteer."

"Were you volun-told to help?"

"No."

"Will you get paid?"

"Nope, I just kinda want to."
My cheeks grow pink.

"If there was an ice cream eating crew,
I'd be into that," Jack says.

I hold my breath, hope he might
offer to stay with me—
choose me, instead of Jade.

When he skates off,
I feel pulled to follow.
I can't blame him
for leaving. It's another
day out of school.

IN LINE

Maybe the only teenager in line,
not sure how I can help or what I can do,
I almost turn and bolt,
but the man in front of me smiles,
and the woman behind me smiles.

Then I hear my name.
"Quinnie!"

It's Ms. Koval, a few people behind me.

"What are you doing here?" I ask.

"Some of my students' homes
were affected—like yours—
so I'm here to help."

"That's nice," I tell her.

"I hope to see you at school
later this week," she says.

When I get to the front of the line,
I put my name down under
Volunteer—and kind of
feel strange for a minute.
The guy organizing doesn't even
ask my age or experience,
explains they're putting together a crew
right now, asks if I have gloves. I say no
and he pulls a new pair from a box.

"Stand over there by that tree,"
he instructs, "and we'll call you
when we have ten people."

DEBRIS CREW

When we reach ten,
we set off for a daycare nearby.
A large tree has collapsed into the house,
and the fence and playground need help.
We meet another crew already at work.

"It's you!" I say, shocked to find Ian,
Weird Old Man's grandson,
on the other crew.

"It's you!" He smiles back.
"Why aren't you working on your own house?"
He leads me to the playground.

"It's mostly stuff I can't do now,
like roofing and window repair.
Why are *you* here?" I ask.

"I want to help my grandpa's neighborhood,"
he says. "And it feels good to help.
Did you know helping others
builds self-esteem? It's a fact."

I'm surprised by
how much older
and wiser he seems
than me.

Ian and I stare
at the swing sets and slide area,
where thousands of pieces of glass
sparkle on the ground like a painful mosaic
for tiny toes and fingers. I think of the glass in my foot.
The owner comes over to us, thanks us, tells us
how a tornado twenty-some years before
took down another tree
and how she's glad
this storm was at night,
so no children were there.

When we don't know where
to begin, she tells us, "Focus
on one square foot at a time."

Ian and I start
picking up the glass,
one shard at a time.

"Where do you go to school?" I ask him.

"I'm a freshman at the arts high school.
Turner," he adds.

I nod, like I know about it.

"I paint, mostly murals—and take photos.
I noticed you like to write.
You should check it out."

But I'm not interested.
I've got other high school plans,
with Jack and Jade.

He tells me about his murals,
about his school and classes.
I find myself leaning toward him,
hanging on every detail.

"Did you paint the mural at your grandpa's?"

"Yeah, that's mine."
He smiles to himself.

"It's good."

I'm surprised when I realize
we've cleared all the glass
from under the swing sets—
and how easy
it is to help.

I capture a torn picture
waving from a fence.
It's a crayon drawing of a family—
two parents, brother, sister, and dog,
standing in front of a square house.
I hold it up to show Ian.

"Raw talent," he proclaims.

We laugh,
and then move on to another area.
"It's like tornados have a dark sense of humor,"
he says. "I saw this tree down
on another street, and there was a
tiny nest with all its blue eggs,
uncracked." He shakes his head
as if it's the most amazing thing.

I smile at this dude
talking about nests and eggs—

        but I like
        his different way
of seeing things.

"Hey, my mom's here," he says.
"See ya soon?"

"Uh, yeah." I watch him walk away,
wonder-hoping if I will.

The owner comes over
when I'm about to head home,
looks me in the eyes, says,
"Fantastic work!"
    And I feel more seen
than I have in weeks.
       Maybe more.

As I walk away,
I think of the daycare babies
and their tiny feet
and how it made *me* feel good,
like Ian said, to help *them*.
I wonder if Mr. Slade would
call this "symbiotic."

FORTY-THREE WATER BOTTLES

On the way back
to my temporary home,
I stop every few feet
and pick up an empty

water bottle, crush it,
and stash it in the grocery bag
another volunteer gave me.
It's weird how people
dropped all these bottles.
Maybe because everything
is already such a wreck.
A few more bottles won't hurt.
But it's something that's
fixable, when so much isn't.

By the time I arrive
back at Ivy Man,
I've collected forty-three.

"VOLUNTEER"

On the seventh day,
I sign up again.
Because I may be unskilled
and untalented, but I'm
discovering I can clean, clear,
sort, and stack gloriously.
And because finding Peevie,
and helping the babies, and picking
up bottles made me feel
valuable.

I can't join a chainsaw crew,
or repair a roof,
but I sign up for possession recovery
and get sent to a house
with five other people.

At the house, we discover
an entire college soccer team
moving bricks from a crumbled wall
to a neat pile
beside the house.

The owners are a family:
a wide-eyed wife and husband,
and a wider-eyed child.
The wife keeps switching the toddler
from one hip to the other.
She leads me into what once was
their living room and says,
"Save anything you can."

I find books and knickknacks
and lay them gently in boxes.
I find a ruined copy of *'Twas the Night
Before Christmas* and imagine them
reading it around a twinkling tree.

Hours later, when I've boxed
this room up, I ask the woman

if she'd like me to play
with the child in the swatch of yard
undisturbed by the storm.
She can't thank me enough.
The little girl drags out a plastic
toy house. She sets up
a bed and couch and people,
then says, "Look!" as she whacks
it with her two tiny fists
and says, "Na-do!"

SORR-JOY-FUL

On the way back to Ivy Man,
I wander past the edge of a yard
where people gather around a fire pit.
A guy is playing guitar, another a stand-up bass,
and a girl is singing a song both sorrowful and joyful,
which is exactly how I feel—sad for the family I helped
who'd lost so much, but happy to be able to help them.
The fire crackles and glows and has pulled the people close.
Everyone is story-sharing. A guy tells me, "Join us,
neighbor." I do the classic look-over-my-shoulder,
but he's talking to me, so I find some undisturbed ground
to sit. Did it take a tornado for people
to come together like this? I lean into the moment,
listen to their versions of the night.

A woman tears up when she describes pulling
her drenched wedding dress from her basement.
A man talks about rescuing his toddler
with a ladder when he couldn't use the stairs.
Everyone is quiet and nodding.
If Jack were here, he'd whisper-cough,
"Cheese-fest." But being here
feels nice, being here
feels right.

CONNECTED AGAIN TO THE OUTSIDE WORLD

Mom calls it a "reprieve" as we leave
the neighborhood in Grandma Jo's car.
She drives to a sandwich shop across town,
an area unharmed by the tornado.
In our dirty clothes, we order dinner
and collapse into a booth. I take out
my notebook and remind her *my* phone
is still lost and my laptop messed up.

While we wait, Mom drums her fingers
and scans her phone. After a few minutes,
she asks—for the first time—about my writing.
For some reason, I tell her, "It's just a project."
But inside I'm glad she's asked, and I can almost
picture—when our house is fixed—hanging
and talking with her at our kitchen table,

like she and Forrest used to do.

For now, she seems relieved when the waiter
interrupts and sets our sandwiches
and drinks between us.

*THE PATH TAKEN

The TV at the sandwich shop
shows a helicopter flying over
the tornado's path. After it arrived,
knocking on the door of our neighborhood,
the tornado whistled its way down a few roads
until it reached the park, which it leaped.
Then it forged a hundred-mile path,
wreaking havoc, on its merry way
to a town just north of us.

Not long ago, Ms. Koval shared a poem
about *a road not taken.** We annotated
and analyzed it, decided it
was about a person with a dilemma
because of a fork in the road.
He has to choose which road to travel.
We discussed how one small decision
can change so much. I think about
choices we made that night—how Mom
woke me and we ran to the basement entry.

How I forgot to save Pumpkin.
But what if most of our decisions
are really made by nature? One house,
or road, or building, or life over another?

*Robert Frost's "The Road Not Taken"

THE WEEK THAT LASTED A YEAR

It's been a week
since the tornado struck.
I swear time has crawled.
It could be the lack of electricity
in our busted home, or moving to Ivy—
days of doing things I've never done,
and all the time spent offline.
Maybe it's just me,
or maybe it's the truce
between Mom and Dad.
But I've changed a lot in the span
of this "week-year."

The After

BACK TO SCHOOL

Mom wakes me when the alarm fails
to do its singular job. Groggily,
I yank on a T-shirt and jeans.
I return equipped with the minimum—
my spiral tucked under my arm
and a pencil tucked inside it.
And brand-new, storm-adjusted,
tornado-opened eyes!

In first period, I really see
the other people around me,
see past the cast of Jack and Jade,
wonder who else's house got hit.
Kiera, with wrinkled clothes like mine?
Lance, who wears the same shirt
and shorts every day? We could
form a new club and call it
the Survivalists.

SECOND PERIOD

Ms. Koval looks my way
more than once,
with her dang kind eyes.
Please don't single me out.
I keep my eyes to myself,
or glance across the classroom at Jack,
doodling on a book.
I wonder if he wonders
what I've been doing at night
since I haven't been
gaming.

Passing out the daily read,
Ms. Koval pauses in front of me.
I count to six in my head.
Finally, she moves on.

"The poem 'Hurricane Rain,'" she tells us,
is about someone who loses their home.
She reads it aloud, and I hang on her
every word, forgetting to read along.
After, she says, "Let's take some time
to process. You don't have to share
how you feel, but you can if you'd like."

Jack's hand shoots up—and before
Ms. Koval can call on him:
"Why would dude sit down and write

this after a hurricane?" He looks around at the class.
"Seems like he should get himself
to Home Depot."

Most of the class laughs,
Jade the loudest.

Ms. Koval nods and sighs—
and tells us, "Due to the recent
storms, I'm extending our thirty days
of poems into May."

To the sound of groans, I raise my hand.
"I wrote a poem about the tornado."
Heads whip my way.

"THE tornado?" someone asks.
"Wonderful," Ms. Koval says.

When she asks us to freewrite
for five minutes in response to "Hurricane Rain," I do
                    and words about the storm and the calm
                    between my parents
                            slide plip-
                                    plop
from my heart
onto the page, filling it up.

But when she asks
for volunteer readers,

I fold my page in half and close it
deep in my spiral, not ready
to share
like that.

"PLEASE STAY AFTER CLASS"

Jack
gives me
the *in trouble* look.
I shake my head, shake it off—
but stand up straight
as everyone
leaves.

Ms. Koval hands me a school laptop
and charger. "You may check this out."

My eyes grow wide.
In touch with the world again!

I take the laptop, hold it
in front of me like a prize,
then something in my brain glitches.
and I pause-in-place,
con-
sid-
er-
ing.

"On second thought"—I can't
believe I'm saying this—"I might
keep writing old-school
on paper—if that's okay?"

"Absolutely," she says.
"Lots of writers write by hand.
You just have to turn your
poems in—and on time."

I like how she lumps me in
with "writers." I smile
and look at my feet,
knowing she gets me—
even my problem
with punctuality.

"You know, Quinnie,
it's okay to be sad
when bad things happen.
Social media—and friends—
might tell you it's all good.
But it's okay if it's not."
She pauses to settle the laptop
back on a shelf and glances
at the picture of herself
with two dogs,
on her desk.

"Keep writing.
It's a safe place for everything you're feeling.
Writing lets you sneak up on the sad stuff.
Maybe you could try writing about your house
or the houses in your neighborhood.
Plenty of poets have written in the POV
of objects to explore their feelings.
My favorite poet once wrote
from the point of view
of a mirror."*

"I did that with my tornado poem!"

"Really?
I'd love to read it."

And I believe her.
"Ms. Koval?"

"Yes." She smiles.

"I promise
to turn my work in
on time—from now on."

*Sylvia Plath's "Mirror"

SEMI-NORMAL

When 11:30 arrives,
I look forward to hot food—
the steaming pizza rectangle,
cup-o-peaches, chocolate milk,
and bag of potato chips—
cafeteria-lunch Heaven!

Jade scrunches her nose
at my tray, peels a banana,
and tells Jack about her
skate competition this Saturday.
She's not just a street skater, like us.
She competes. And wins.

Jack eats up her words.

The principal is making rounds
and small talk with students,
mostly tornado kids. She stops
at our table and smiles at me,
tells the whole table, "Anyone
who had textbooks damaged
won't be held responsible."

Jack is quick: "Dr. Williams,
the tornado ruined all my books
and my homework too!"

"You wish!"
She winks at him.

I'm glad she has a big heart
for Jack; she always has.
Maybe she knows about his dad.

"Naw, but for real," he says,
like he's talking to a friend,
"Quinnie's house got hit."

After lunch, she calls me
and Kiera and a couple others over.
We follow her to a storage room,
where she pulls backpacks from a box,
hands me a floral one—which is,
like I said, floral—but better
than my ruined one.

BUS RIDE BACK INTO TORNADO-VILLE

We see it from a new angle:
notice how a random line seems
to divide those hit and those safe—
houses and businesses here:
perfectly fine. And there:
they're just not. The line begins
at the interstate overpass,

the place where Jack and I hang,
hoping one of the cars is carrying his dad
back home to him.

I can almost pretend I live in
one of the undamaged houses, or Jack's sturdy
stone home, which wasn't touched,
except a few flowerpots,
swept off the porch.

The destruction mesmerizes—I am
dazed by what once was—the ice cream parlor,
the bar and restaurant, the post office,
the firehouse, and then house after house
after house
after house
after house
after house.

When I start writing,
Jack leans over to talk to me.
"Homework's for losers," he scoffs.
(I don't tell him I have to write
before the details in my head are lost.)
"Wanna do mine?" he says.
And eventually, "Bor-ing!"
He shrugs, gives up,
and turns away.

BRAINSTORM

No rain in *this* storm—
just ideas and words
and sun from a bus window
on my skin—so warm it feels
like I'm plugged in, charging,
solar-powered: images
of torn-up houses swirl by and
their **voices** pop into my head
so quickly my hand can't keep up.
I don't know if what I'm writing
is good or worth sharing—
but the more I write,
the more my mood lifts.
Writing a new forecast,
with a brand-new outlook
for me and my neighbors,
writing a paper world
of distance between us
and anything that threatens.

A CHORUS OF HOUSES

We, houses, know things.
We have our avenues, connected
through sewer and power lines.
We swap stories with
misdelivered mail, like seeds

in the air between yards, like dogs
without fences. Sometimes,
we can't help ourselves
and whisper hints to our new residents,
drop clues beneath wallpaper,
or trinkets of those who came before
in vents. We do our best
to closet your family's secrets,
curtained and shuttered away,
in basements and attics.
You might never know
what's going on in a home.
You catch loose
snippets across yards,
or words from door to car,
or through our open windows.
But we see it all—
the love, the births, the fights,
the loneliness, the death.
After the storm, you walk
in wonder at the secrets spilled:
"He was a painter?"
when you see ruined canvases
hanging in a roofless studio.
Oh, but we knew! We knew.
Or, "Look at all her stuff,"
when you learn she never threw
anything away after he left.
Sometimes we grow weary
with the weight of it on our

floors and frames, sometimes we take it
with us when we are demolished.
Oh—what we have witnessed!

CLUES

Back at Ivy,
I climb Mr. Jones's stairs,
softly knock, then knock louder still.
Mom left our apartment locked,
with no key under the mat—
as if getting to work was her
sole agenda over everything else.

The muffled, creaky voice:
"Come in!" matches the creaking
door as I enter. A one-dog
committee bounds to greet me
wagging and wiggling. It's nice
to be welcomed by Freddie,
who whines for pats, until I place
a single one on his head.

"In here," Mr. Jones calls
from a room off the kitchen.
I tiptoe that way. "Excuse me?
Sir? I'm locked out."

I'm surprised to find him

reading a book and chuckling
to himself, laughing with no one
else around. Jack would
call that wack.
But I'm curious
about the book
AND
he tells me to sit,
so I sit and Freddie obeys too
and sits at Mr. Jones's feet.

We watch him read.

How long does he expect me
to watch him read a book?

Finally, he carefully bookmarks
his spot and smiles.

When he notices me watching,
he points to a small stack
of books carefully organized
on the table beside him.
"Mrs. Jones had chosen ten
she planned for us to read together.
I'm on book number eight."
He sighs and eventually
maneuvers from his chair.
"Follow me," he says,
as if he's just remembered

I need something.

We make our way—s-l-o-w-l-y—
downstairs, where he lets me into
the apartment. There I discover
another surprise—a solitary
business card, haphazard-ish,
on the floor like trash.
I stare at it. *D-i-v-o-r-c-e Attorney,*
it reads back: Tracy Cox, Esq.

HOPEFUL

Maybe the card
was here before
we moved in.
I step over it and
head out back, leave
the stupid basement,
which is not my home,
without questioning the business
of that stupid business card.
I sit outside, doing math,
hoping for a C, but mostly
staring into the setting sun,
letting my eyes blink
                    blink
            blink
                    and close

for a few minutes—

then Mom and Dad arrive on scene
holding my report card
between them, they kiss and hug—
which should've been the clue
that stirred me back to reality,
because instead of doing math
I am
dozing—
and
dreaming.

FOUND POEM

Today, Ms. Koval teaches us
that a found poem
is based on words
you find, like
on a bathroom wall

b yourself
or
i just wrote on a wall

or on a cereal box

heart healthy
and
daily dose

I will NOT quote words
from the business card
I found.

Instead, the words I discover
are from a faded list
stuffed in a bush
in our front yard
begging me
to share its story.

THE LIST

Wherever you are, I hope you remember your *power greens,*
raisins, cilantro & Roma tomatoes from the list the tornado
snatched from your purse or car, your counter, your table,
sent sailing in the dark with bricks and shingles,
gutters and stop signs, that flung insulation into power lines,
that whipped a trampoline into a tree, that tumbled houses
like toys, that left so many without a home, without a counter
on which to put a list. That left me unsure of what to do,
until someone told me, "Focus on one square foot at a time."

I could buy the items on your list—*cinnamon, milk, eggs*—
and walk them to your door—if I knew where you lived.
And what about your door? Is it there?
Or piled on the mountain of rubble and wood,
or the pieces of houses lining curbs,
just steps from my own home.

In one corner, you'd scribbled *salad for dinner*.
Your list from Sunday or Monday that by Tuesday
would have been revised to gloves, tarps, and duct tape,
to rakes and two-by-fours, to nails, and a new broom—
things you didn't know you'd need. How could you know
that you'd have no roof under which to make
a nourishing salad of power greens?

THIS IS NOT A EULOGY

Ms. Koval told me
to write about hard things
by sneaking up on them,
so I'm not going to write
about Pumpkin being dead.
Instead, I will recall his pointy ears,
white whiskers and claws,
his stubby tail and caramel-swirled fur,
his silly cheek pouches and round haunches.
I will not imagine him forever-gone
or consider what might have happened.
Instead, I will write that hamsters have 124 bones,

thinner than matchsticks, thinner than dogwood
twigs bending in the wind. I will describe
his heartbeat against my palm like a tiny clock,
how I freshen his cedar chips daily, supply
clean water, and scatter seeds in his cage,
leaving the door wide open
for him to come back home.

DROP-BY #2

Jade's mom drops her off at Jack's
to "do homework" most afternoons now,
but when she drives away, they hop
on their boards, set off.

Sometimes I see them fly by.

Today they drop by Ivy to find me—
since I'm not working on my house.
I'm striking a "doing homework" pose
when they skate up the alley, wheels
popping on loose gravel. I can't help but feel uncertain
when they appear, and I look toward the windows,
willing Mr. Jones to stay inside—'cause you never know
what Jack will do or say when he thinks
adults are out of listening range.

They leap the small fence,
pull up chairs on either side of me,
and place their boards on the iron patio table.

"Make yourself at home," I laugh.

"You know we will," Jack smacks back,
then commands, "Come skate with us."

When I don't jump up—
"So, this is your new spot?" Jade asks,
skeptically scanning the place.

"Temporary," I explain.
"We're moving back home soon."

"Creepy!" She stands, already bored,
and finds a stick to poke stuff: the potted
plants Ian nurtures, an anthill,
the holes in the fence.

"You *do* know who lives here, Quinnie?" Jack asks.

"Duh!"
I glance at the door.

Jack raises his eyebrows,
tells Jade, "This old dude is
like ninety-nine percent most likely the guy

who nabbed that missing
girl twenty years ago."

"He's not that bad," I say,
hoping that's the end of that.
"And his grandson is pretty cool."

"Creepy dude's grandson? Ew!" Jade says.

Jack shoots me a look.
"That why you're avoiding us? Ian?"
He pronounces his name
like it's foul in his mouth.

"No. I barely know him.
It's my house. And homework."
I don't mention that I might prefer
to write.

"Man, you sound like Forrest!"
Jack says—and then, "We'll wait.
You can't choose that stuff over us."
He taps the table loudly while Jade
makes a beat with the stick.

Like I have no other option,
I scribble answers
for the last six problems.

PLAYGROUNDS

The three of us walk
in the middle of the street,
heading into the sunset, climbing
the hill on Holly, laughing and joking.
For a moment, it feels like old times,
like before, and I can't get enough.
We are invincible among
the destruction!

What was I thinking
choosing math over this?
If I subtract myself from this friendship—
what's left?

Jack calls the neighborhood "our playground,"
with the streetlights knocked out,
and the roads blocked off, and the houses
and businesses abandoned—
even though police cars still idle on corners,
warning lights on, to prevent looting.
Jack shouts, "They can't stop *us!*"

I picture the playground in City Park
where Jack and I once played as toddlers.
Then when we grew, the parents
of smaller humans had to shoo us off.

At dusk, we pause at the top of the hill,
surveying the damage.
Jack materializes a can
of neon-green spray paint—
a look of intent crosses his face.

"What for?" I ask.

"That house!" He points
to a house I'd passed a zillion times before,
a house now half smashed,
with glass jutting like broken teeth
from a gaping mouth
after a schoolyard fight.

At that moment
               something inside me shifts.
I stop walking, stop soaring,
start coming down fast, staring
at the ruined house
that still
       belongs
               to someone,
                       someone just like me.

Jack sprays a big face on its porch,
runs back to us, tosses the can to Jade,
who sprints to the house,
looks around for witnesses,
and then sprays her initials
across its front door.

She returns, tosses the can to me.
"Your turn!" she squeals.

They both wait, watch.
                "Or not . . ."
Jade sounds annoyed now.

"The house is busted, Quinnie," Jack says.

"But what if they're going to fix it?"

"So lame," Jade says. "Come on, Jack!"
She starts off on her board
down the hill. Jack starts to follow,
and it feels like they're walking
away for good.

"Wait—" I call after them, shake the can,
and paint a set of eyes onto
a remaining window—
but every
            moment of it
                        feeling like I suck
                                    especially when

                                    I glimpse a woman
                                    through the window in
                                    the backyard, sorting
                                    through stuff.

GHOST OF A GIRL

"Gotta split,"
I tell Jack and Jade a minute later
and run-walk away. They call after me—
but I can't turn around.

In an alley,
I discover a little girl's dress
        flapping in a half-uprooted tree
dressed to impress
by a tornado parent.

In surprise, I stare at it,
imagining the little girl
wearing it, for Easter or her birthday.
I wonder if she wonders
where it is—this missing piece
of her childhood,
now waving like a ghost
of a girl. Or maybe
that's just how
I feel.

NEON-GREEN-HANDED

Mom hits me with questions:
"Where've you been?

It's dark, past dinnertime.
Were you with Jack?
Your math book was
just sitting out back."

I've never been good at lying,
and she spots my hands.

"What's that?"
Disappointment settles
on her lips.

I don't answer.
I could've been volunteering.
I have no energy for a defense, so I shove
the evidence in my pockets.

"Quinn, the tornado
gave you a little leeway,
but you need to fix your grades
before high school.
Should I call school
and have you put
in a new study hall?"

She's been threatening this all year,
to separate me from Jack,
to improve my grades.

This time, I don't argue.
It's pointless—I'm already losing
Jack to Jade, and to everything I'm not.

"Maybe you two need a break.
He's becoming a bad influence.
Talk to me before you
hang out with him again.
And where's your report card?"

Honestly, I'm surprised
she even noticed, since she has
a crammed-full calendar
with very little *me* on it.
With luck, my report card
was at the post office
hit by the tornado.

HAIKU-NOTE TO FUTURE PARENTS

If you want your kid
to do something, simply tell
them *not* to do it.

SMASHING THINGS

Passing tests
isn't a talent of mine,

so when Jack calls,
I jump—yet again.
Looks like I passed
the spray paint test.

"Check this out," Jack says,
then throws a rock and smashes
the top pane of a window.

Same song.
Different day.
I drag my feet
and lag behind.

"Goal!" Jade sings
triumphantly.

A stone in your hand
doesn't feel that different
from a baseball or football,
a horseshoe or Frisbee.
Similar energy.
Different possibility.

There's an in-between
when a friendship is coming unglued—
but you haven't found
the new you.

What do I have to lose?

The stone is smooth
and round. I scooped it
from their yard.
Maybe the family found it
on a hike. Maybe it lined
a flower bed. Maybe the child
who lived here believed
it was a magic bean, pirate coin,
or superpower pellet.

To me, a stone
is like a choice,
heavy in my hands.

Jade and Jack walk over,
stand on either side of me,
waiting. The house is vacant,
I tell myself, it will be
demolished,
I tell myself,
it is not mine.

"Waiting!" Jade says.

I raise my arm, take aim,
and let the stone leave
my grip. It sails through air,
lands square in the pane
of an upstairs window.

The shatter is momentarily
beautiful.

Then I feel something else.

Regret.

TREASURE OR TRASH?

On the way home,
I discover an entire box
of half-used spray paints,
probably dumped
from someone's shed.

Like an old habit,
I stash them
in my floral backpack.
Jade and Jack would freak
if they saw
my score—
      but I may not
            show it to them.

THE NEXT MORNING, I SPY

a piece of drywall
against a wrecked fence.

I can't help but see it
as a blank page.
I guess Ian would see it
as a canvas for a mural,
like the one
he painted
in Ivy.

I think about it all day.
The cans in my backpack rattle,
beg me to show them off,
or present them to Jack
and claim best friend status back,
but I shush them, compose
words and lines
in my head instead.

"What's new, Q?" he asks,
at lunch, like he doesn't care
if I respond or not, then says, "Good talk,"
and turns to Jade
when I stay in my mind
and don't have much to say.

In science, Mr. Slade,
wearing a Hawaiian shirt,
reminds us to recycle
our old lab reports.

"Do we get a grade for that?" Jade asks.

Mr. Slade chuckles. "My dear, it's called
being a global citizen," then he rambles
about something called the butterfly effect
and the flapping of a butterfly's wings
causing a catastrophic weather event
halfway across the world.

The class stares blankly.
But he has my attention.
And something inside me clicks.
I will not give the paint to Jack.
The canvas and I have a date.

That afternoon, I walk
                              back
                                        to the drywall,
glance around,
and paint these words

> *Stay strong.*
> *We survived!*
> *Hold that vibe.*
> *Hear the song*
> *Of lives resuming*
> *And hope blooming.*

I pause for a moment,
think about a poem

we read in class by a poet
by the name of Emily,*
then push the nozzle again
and sign the poem like this:

   —*Nobody*

*Emily Dickinson's "I'm Nobody! Who are you?"

AFTERGLOW

Freddie's outside
when I arrive at Ivy.
He says hello with licks—
and I don't push him away
this time.

I flop into a chair
and recite my poem
out loud to him.

He lifts his face
like he's proud of me.
Glad someone is.

Pumpkin had three
emotions: neutral,
hyped-up-all-night,
and scared.

I place my hand
upon Freddie's head.
He wags his tail and lounges
at my feet, basking
in the afterglow
of my touch.

A few minutes later,
Mr. Jones comes out,
carrying Freddie's bowls.
Freddie bolts over
and tails him to the spigot,
where Mr. Jones,
who does not see me,
says, "Hello, my boy,
Frederick," while carefully
washing Freddie's bowls.
Freddie sits at his feet,
listening, watching
Mr. Jones. I think about
announcing myself,
maybe asking about his book,
but there's something
private and sweet
about their interaction.

PERSON-IFYING

Sometimes I think
we don't see each other clearly.
Like I would've never seen
the book-reading side
of Mr. Jones if it weren't for
Mom locking me out.

Or take Ms. Koval.
She's more than a teacher—
like with a home and bed
and non-teacher clothes,
and cereal in her cabinet.

I know she drinks a smoothie
most days for lunch. And
she's friends with the principal.
And she looks at the picture
of the dogs on her desk a lot.

Today she taught us the meaning
of *anthropomorphize*.
Well, sort of taught us.
She ended class by saying:
"Make the dictionary your friend,
my friends." And so I did.

Turns out, dictionaries are people too—
and very good friends
to writers.

THE STORY OF A HOUSE PART I

Once upon a time, a house was born. I'd been empty for so long
when they came up my walk. The children skipped between
the parents, like a picture you'd hang on a wall. I wanted to be
in that picture, even just in the background. When their feet
touched my porch, I held my breath. The porch swing creaked
like a welcome song. They rang my doorbell and wiped their
feet; I took that as a sign. The children, *Forrest* and *Quinnie,*
they were called, ran from room to room. Their voices echoed in
my emptiness. In the kitchen, *Mom* turned on the sink. I rushed
cold water through my pipes to meet her hands. She looked out
the window and sighed. All four squeezed into the bathroom. I
imagined the good times we'd have. In the middle of the hallway,
Dad kissed *Mom* on the head. The children yelled, "Family
hug!" and I was sold; I was theirs—the Nash Family House! We,
houses, are more than a place to hang a hat and park a car. We
measure our lives in families—and I'd found mine.

IF I WERE FORREST

When Mom arrives,
she finds me in bed, writing,

legs propped up on the wall,
attempting another point-of-view poem,
like Ms. Koval suggested.

Mom asks about the house,
about Dad's progress.

I sit up instantly
to crisscross applesauce.
"He's working on your bedroom,
installing that closet lighting
you've always wanted,"
I tell her.

I study her face,
analyze the emotion
hidden there like the theme
of a thick novel.

She blinks, then changes the subject
to her job, an upcoming coffee date
with a colleague in a different part
of the city. That must be her way
of escaping what the tornado
has done. Or maybe
she's escaping something else—
like me
or Dad.

She and Forrest
used to hang in our kitchen
at night, talking endlessly. Right now,
she wants to tell me something
but can't find the words. I think
of the business card I found.

"So, Quinn, I found the cans
of paint in your bag."

"What were you doing in my bag?"

"You dropped it in the middle
of the floor. I heard the rattle
when I moved it."

Caught. Again.
Clearly, I'm no
expert on stealth.

"What are they for?"
She wants me to explain.

When I don't know how to,
she says, "A change might
be good for you, for these
last six weeks of school.
It might help your grades,
help you focus on what's
important. Besides—I've

already made the call
and requested a change
to your study hall."

I stare wide-eyed.
If I were Forrest, she'd believe
the cans were for a service project,
for a class presidential campaign,
for anything *other* than
being up to no good.

CRUM-
B
L
I
N
G—AGAIN

Mom calls Dad on her cell.
From the other bedroom of the apartment,
I can hear most of the argument.
Her volume raised to sharing mode—
and walls like crepe paper.

First, it's about insurance,
then our house, then me,
then them.

I hope to hear him soften,
but his voice matches hers
like a competition.

I build a mental wall,
pull the covers over my face,
start composing rhymes
and lines in my mind
to drown them out:

> *Build a wall*
> *Stumble*
> *Bumble*
> *Crumble*
> *Fall*
> *Forget it all*
> *Forget it all*

GRANDMA JO TALKS ABOUT STRENGTH

Dad brings Grandma Jo over
for a backyard sit at Ivy Man,
so we can "shoot the breeze,"
as Grandma says. He leaves
to go work on the house
without speaking to Mom.

Today is a good day
for Grandma, whose speech
is clear, and she's "with-it,"
although she leans on things
when she walks and
is weaker since I last saw her.

When it's only the two of us,
Grandma asks how I'm doing—
she seems to mean more
than with our house. I shake
my head, as if I don't know.

"You know," she says,
"you're not *just* named after me,
Quinn Jolene Nash. You
take after me. You're strong."
And she sounds strong
when she says it.

Can she tell
I don't feel it, hanging my head,
kicking pebbles at my feet?
She reaches over
and pats my knee.

"You could come live with me and"—
she pauses—"in the country."

She doesn't say "with your dad,"
but I fill in the blanks in my head.

"Wouldn't it be a hoot
if you went to your dad's high school?"

For a split second—
when I picture Jack and Jade learning
I've been moved out of study hall
because they're quote-unquote
"bad influences"—I actually
consider it.

"THE IRONY KILLS ME"

Ian visits his grandpa again.
Together, we walk Freddie
across to the dog park.

"I'll be out here." I keep space
between me and the herds: chunky
slobbering dogs, dogs with hidden eyes,
old ones sniffing the yippy,
darting dogs—and Freddie
in the mix of it all.

Ian aims his camera at the humans
standing distanced, tracking
and following their dogs.

"The dogs are that way," I call
to him, pointing.

He comes and leans on the fence.
"The irony kills me," he says.
"They bring their dogs to socialize
but don't talk to each other."

"You're an odd one," I say.
But when his smile slips,
I add, "In a good way.

"What do you do with all
these photos of strangers?"

"I look for one that tells a story."
Then he turns the camera on me.
"What story do you want
your picture to tell?"

MS. KOVAL TALKS ABOUT RHYME

"Our ears like it, anticipate, and wait
for a full or slant rhyme to come along,

completing the first one.
Rhymes can complete an idea
or a feeling," she explains.

I write this down—
but stop writing when I spy
Jade staring—
or glaring.

"They help babies learn
language, as they predict sounds
in their heads. Think about
picture books and songs."

I think of the church's steeple
still sitting in the road
and the nursery rhyme

> *Here's the church.*
>> *Here's the steeple.*
>>> *Open it up*
>>>> *and see all the people.*

So many churches
in my neighborhood
are opened up to the sky.
One is missing two of its four walls.
You can see into the church and through
its stained glass. The rows of pews
are still lined up, holding
Bibles and hymnals.

Jack says from across the room,
"Like, there once was a man named Chuck, who—"

"That's enough!" Ms. Koval says sharply.

"Put your rhymes on paper,
Mr. Edwards, and then you can
read them at our coffeehouse
at the end of May."

"I don't drink coffee," Jack says.

Ms. Koval gives him a warning look,
which means she's probably
planning to call his mom.

SCHOOL RULES PART II, ACCORDING TO JACK

According to Jack,
always *Go for the laugh!*
Even if it earns you
a phone call home.

Stunts Jack has pulled lately:
hide Ms. Koval's remote for her screen,
try to flush the bathroom pass, tear out
the final page of everyone's book,
steal the last ten pieces of the thousand-piece

puzzle on the back table. And today—
he "misplaced" Ms. Koval's picture
of the two dogs and her. I don't know why—
but I laugh along with the class.
It's eighth grade—laugh
or be laughed at.

This last prank makes
Ms. Koval
get
really
really
quiet.

FEELING SORRY AFTER CLASS

I stay back, wanting to say,
I'm sorry for Jack. And for laughing, but I can't
find the right words. Ms. Koval sits at her desk,
which she rarely does, staring at the place
her picture usually stands.

"Are they your dogs?" I ask.

"They *were* mine, once upon a time.
When my boyfriend and I split up,
it made more sense for him to keep them."

I don't know how to reply,
but I think about Pumpkin.
And Mom and Dad.

Ms. Koval looks up after a beat, takes off her
glasses, sits back in her chair, folds her hands
in her lap, and gives me her full attention,
something no one has done in a while.

I soak it up.

"So . . . I heard about this high school," I start,
pushing away my other thoughts.
"This kid Ian told me about it.
It's all about the arts."

"Ah—You mean Turner School of the Arts?"

"I was wondering what you know about it."

"Well, I know it takes a *complete* portfolio,
an audition, and a teacher's recommendation."
She sounds tired—and less
patient than usual.

"The application process—it's a lot.
You'd have to really want it, Quinnie."

I think of my track record,
of my grades in other subjects,
of laughing with the class.

And in that moment,
I don't ask for a recommendation.
I'm too busy grabbing my floral backpack.
"Okay, thanks." Maybe I don't have
what it takes, maybe I'm not
poet material.

MR. JONES TALKS ABOUT WORDS

"What are you writing there?"
Mr. Jones putters around the patio.
We've gotten awkwardly comfortable
in each other's company.

"Nothing—just some words."
I think of Ms. Koval telling me
it takes a *complete portfolio*—

"Nothing, huh?" He dumps
water from a bucket into the ground,
with Freddie one step behind.
"Young lady"—he clears his throat
as if prepping for a sermon—
"words are *not* nothing. They

are everything. In fact,
words save lives."

He emphasizes these last three words.

I roll my eyes behind his back,
but maybe he senses it, because he stops
and bends to sit. "You don't believe me?"

He waits, but I don't know what to say,
his sincerity catches me off guard.

"Let me tell you about a time
when words saved lives."

I sigh and give him half of my attention.

"I was a career bus driver.
Had been driving the same route
with the same passengers for near twenty years,
and this one gentleman—Andy—he
was having a year. He'd lost his wife
to cancer, then lost his job, but he kept
riding the bus each day anyway.
It was his routine."

Mr. Jones pauses to see if I'm listening.

I am listening.

"Then one morning, he had—what they call
these days a mental health emergency.
Sorry to say, he pulled a weapon on me
and the other passengers."

I close my spiral.

"I talked to him then—
told him I saw him, knew him, that he
didn't want to hurt us. That was not him.
Then I listened to his words.
He was so hurt and angry with life.
After a while, Andy calmed down."

"Wow," I say. "What happened to him?"

"Well, he went to jail for it. But years later,
he found me, had a little boy with him.
Told me he was married again and happy.
Told me *my words* saved *his* life—
saved all our lives that day."

This is the most Mr. Jones has ever talked.

I sit thinking about his story.
I sit pondering the power of words.
I sit wishing I'd said *I'm sorry*
to Ms. Koval.

NEIGHBORHOOD SOUNDTRACK—EXTENDED VERSION

Before the tornado, it was a symphony of birds, horns,
sirens, the hum of traffic on the interstate, a ball game
in City Park, laughter, someone calling their dog.
*Hello!*s & *How are ya?*s, people talking to themselves,
people talking on phones, church bells,
bar music, and the chat-happy restaurant crowds.

Now, day into night, just a few weeks out, the instrumental
is sawing, hammering, drilling, buzzing, and cutting.

I wouldn't have noticed these as songs—if it weren't for
this poetry project, which is changing everything—
even the very composition of me.

SUDDENLY EVERYTHING

Suddenly everything is a blank page
like the sky for a skywriting plane.
I find a garage door torn from a house.
A table in the alley missing its legs.
A single brick wall left standing,
once belonging to a mattress store.
No one will mind a poem here or there,
so I spray my words carefully:

Neighbors,
You got this!
Persist! Recover!
Rebuild!
        —Nobody

I feel more like a new *Quinn*
than *Nobody* when I'm painting
my poem this time.

NATURAL CONSEQUENCES

Mom brings me back down to earth
when she shows me her screen:
an email from my math teacher.

I make no case for myself.
I can't be a straight-A student, even if
I turn everything in.

    The school gets around to
    arranging my new schedule,
    and I'm banished
from my study hall, which is no minor thing
in the delicate ecosystem of eighth grade.

Jack and Jade and everyone else
watch me gather up my stuff,

dropping books from my locker
to the floor and shuffling it all
into my floral backpack.
I glance at Jack, already turning
to talk with Jade. I think to myself
He's all yours.
No one waves. They stare,
relieved it's not them.

In my new classroom,
which turns out to be Ms. Koval's,
the others eye me like I'm a predator
come to rush their food supply.
They turn away, so I don't sit or take
what they have claimed.

Ms. Koval makes a seat for me
and clears a locker for my things.
I use the alone time to type up
some of the poems I like best.

I even take a chance and email
three of them to Forrest.

PEP-LESS RALLY

It's Friday,
and we are marched

into the gym single file.
School spirit is the last feeling I feel.
I'm wondering who I will sit by—
those in front or behind me?
I could break rank and sit by Kiera,
who always smiles at me in art,
but Ms. Koval is firm and instructs us,
"Stay in line!"

We trudge to the top row,
semi-obediently, except Jamari,
who swipes the leg of a kid
in front of him. Within seconds,
teachers descend, put a stop
to the eighth-grade horseplay. I can't escape,
so I squish between a guy
with BO and Jamari.
Everyone gets on their phones,
begins laughing and joking,
as if sitting all day
has unleashed the wild in us.

What do you do with your body
during a pep rally? I could be clap-silly
like the fifth graders clumped
in a bleacher across from us.
I decide my hands are interesting,
until I pick out Jade and Jack two rows up
and over from me. Through the noise,

I hear them loud-talking about plans
for his birthday. Not sure if Jack sees
me or what—do I wave?

Instead, I study the gym teacher
who's running the whole show.
He draws names from a cap—
"Jade Williamson, come on down!"

The eighth grade erupts
like she's a shooting star.
Kids high-five her on her way there.
Louder than anyone,
Jack chants:

> *Jade!*
> *Jade!*
> *Jade!*

I remember when
he supported
me like that.

It's an obstacle course.
And Jade represents the eighth grade.
If she wins, we win the spirit stick
for the year. I guess
it's a big deal, because
everyone jumps to their feet
and starts screaming and chanting

and stomp,
       stomp,
              stomping.

Jade versus a tall seventh grader,
all muscles and confidence.

Long story short, Jade
puts him in his place—
in other words, kills it.

RE-

We return to study hall
for the last ten minutes of the day.
I've never felt so alone.
I stay at my desk,
open my spiral and pretend to write
pretend not to tear up
pretend not to care—until
                    Ms. Koval calls me to her desk,
casting a brighter spotlight
with her bright smile
on me.

I have trouble focusing
and comprehending her words,
but she is holding one of my poems
in her hands. In other classes,

I tend to collect phrases
like *Redo it. Rework it.*
Resubmit it.

But she describes my poem
as *reflective,* I think, and maybe even says
remarkable and *one for the portfolio,*
but I'll need to replay her words
in my head later
when I'm alone
and can think.

ON THE BUS

Jack flashes his student ID at the driver,
sits down beside Jade, two seats in front of me,
tosses his backpack and board in the seat
between us. Doesn't even turn
his head my way.

Whatever.

When we're almost home,
I hear them laugh the words *pep rally* and *kicked his butt.*
Jack looks over his shoulder.
"Didn't see you there, Quinnie,"
and then turns back to Jade,
who points out the window at a house
with one window left intact.

"Ten bucks," she says,
"I can get it in one try."

"Why, though," I mutter under my breath.

"Were you talking to us?" she says flatly.

"Maybe."

"I thought we weren't good enough.
Isn't that why you left our study hall?"
She glances at Jack for approval.

"Just trying to pass classes,
and Ms. Koval is helping me
with my writing."
It's easy to lie.

"So . . . you're a poet now?" Jade laughs.

(Maybe I'm more than that—
or maybe that's enough.)
But I ignore her question.
"You don't even know who lives there."

"No one lives there now," Jack says.

"It could be my house."

"It's not."

"It's still somebody's," I insist.

"They moved out, Quinnie," Jade says,
somehow making *Quinnie* sound like *Baby*.

"You guys don't get it!"
I'm almost in tears now.
Like a baby.

"And you don't get us anymore, Quinnie,"
Jack says, anger thick in his voice.
"Besides, your mom told my mom
that I'm a bad influence."

I shake my head in shock.
"You think I wanted to lose
all my stuff and live
in that stupid house?"
But when I say it, the word *stupid*
feels wrong.

"Then be with us," Jack says.
"Jade is getting off
at my house today."

"I can't," I say, standing too early
for my stop.

I get off anyway

and walk the rest of the block to Ivy,
tears streaking my face.

"FRIEND"

In the backyard, I run into Ian
and Freddie—because there's no place
to be alone when a tornado
has stolen your home.

"Hello, Fred." I swipe my face
with my sleeve and don't
look up to meet Ian's eyes.

"Hello, friend," Ian says.

I can feel him studying me,
and then he bows goofily,
like he's trying to cheer me up.

I can't help but smirk
but also pen a mental note
on how he called me friend.

"You want to take a walk?"

When I hesitate,
he holds up Freddie's leash—
and Freddie starts wiggling
uncontrollably.

I shake my head and give in.
"How could we disappoint
Prince Freddie?"

In the park, not far away, Jack and Jade
arrive, skating and fake-not-seeing me.
Jack's getting almost as good as Jade.

Noticing me watching them,
Ian asks, "You skate?"

This boy's perceptive!

"That's a matter of opinion,"
I say in my smartass-cautious-
ready-to-joke-or-be-defensive way.

He waits patiently
for a real answer.

"Yeah, I skate," I confirm,
feeling more like myself
with him.

"It's a great mode of transportation
and good for the environment," he tells me.

"Sure—" I laugh, despite myself.
I study Jack and Jade
across the way, not
studying me back.
And the tears almost reappear.

"I bet you're pretty good, Quinn."

He calls me Quinn for some reason this time—
and it feels right when he says it.

I almost forget about Jack and Jade
as we walk back to Ivy,
Freddie pulling the leash,
and Ian's free arm
swinging between us,
my hand inches from his.

"Look"—Ian points to the steeple
still on the edge of the street—
"the church has lost its hat."

I wait for the joke—
but it's just his observation.

I think about telling him
about the poems I've been writing.

"I like how you see things," I tell him instead,
"and then you just say them."

"Isn't that what people do?" He laughs,
flopping his hair off his face.

"You'd be surprised," I say.
The differences between Jack
and Ian make me feel something
I can't explain—like crying and laughing
tumbled together, and like everything
I've ever known is about to change.

Ian asks me to hold Freddie's leash.
He pulls his camera from his backpack,
aims, focuses, and takes a picture
of the steeple. "Documenting,"
he tells me, and I realize
that's partly why
I've been writing.

Documenting.

"THE STEEPLE'S POV"
FOR IAN BY QUINN

People arrive from all over
to view me, the steeple—
like a hat blown from a head
during a fierce gust. I landed
point side up, in the middle

of the street, where worshippers
and strangers stand and pose,
like I'm the latest fashion.
Until I'm hoisted back up
to where I belong, atop a chapel
dressed in its Sunday best,
full of rejoicing, happy people
who fill it up with song.

WHAT'S IN A PSEUDONYM?

Ms. Koval reminds us,
"*Pseudo* means false
and *nym* means name."
While she's explaining,
I think to myself:

> *I'm afraid to want it, but*
> *I want to be a writer—*

even after this project is over.

Maybe writing could be my expertise.

I've begun to feel more like Quinn
than Quinnie or Quinn(ie)
when I'm writing, like a better,
more capable me.

I did some research on pseudonyms—
George Eliot chose hers
to avoid stereotypes,
and the author of *Little Women*
went by Flora Fairfield at first, because
she felt she was still developing.

If writing is thinking,
as Ms. Koval says,
I'm going to keep
write-thinking
on who
I mean
to be.

REVISION

In study hall, I rework lines, crafting the lie
I told Jack and Jade into truth by working
on my poetry with Ms. Koval nearby.

In a penciling trance, tuning others out,
my headspace fills with words and sounds.
Ms. Koval startles me when she asks,
"How's the poetry coming along?"

I shrug, consider how Forrest
finally emailed me back,
said, "Let's talk about these

when I get back." I imagine he plans
to give me advice on how to bring them
up to the Forrest gold standard.

"I've been doing what you said—
trying to write about houses and things,
like maybe for a portfolio.
I'm just not happy with them yet."

"Here," she says, and hands me
a stack of printouts, "help me hang
these up for National Poetry Month—
better late than never."

She nods at the poems in my hands.
"Each of these has probably been revised
countless times. Few writers
get the words right on their first try.
Writing, as you're learning, is a process."

Then she goes all teacher mode:
"Did you know the word *revise*
comes from *vise*, which means to see?
Like *vision, visualize,* and *envision.*
So *revise* literally means
to see again, or to see anew,
like for the very first time."

I nod.

I know she's talking about writing,
but I start to wonder
if you can *revise* yourself too.
See yourself in a new light
and not through the lens
of a forever-more-successful brother,
forever-joking
maybe former best friend,
and forever-fighting
mom and dad.

Ms. Koval asks me
to hang a few of the poems in the hallway
outside her classroom, so I do.
I go in to get more tape,
and behind her door,
I find Jack's jacket
without Jack in it.

JACK'S JACKET

I'm learning that
sometimes an object
is more than an object—
more like our feelings about an object
or memories attached to it.
"A symbol," Ms. Koval says.

I bring the jacket to Jack's
study hall. Ask Mr. Slade
if I can give it to him.
Jack meets me at the door,
cuts a glance over his shoulder
to Jade and some other kids.

It might be
a smelly, dirty jacket,
but to Jack—I know—
it's everything.

Camo can't
hide or disguise
that from me.

I hand it
to him and he scoffs,
"It's hot, I don't need that,"
and tosses it toward his locker,
where it lands
on the floor.

"NOT MY HOUSE ANYMORE"

After school, Dad assigns me
the task of carting roof shingles
and chunks of cut-up dogwood

to our rented dumpster squatting
on what used to be the flower bed
Dad planted last spring.

I take trips back

and

      forth

with the wobbly-but-dependable wheelbarrow,
tossing pieces of tree
up
     and
          over
             the edge.

On one trip, I find him
on a break in the shade
of a remaining tree, examining
his beat-up hands.

I flop down beside him.

"Seems like this will
go on forever," he complains.

"But our house is looking good," I insist.

"Lotta damage you can't see—
and I'm putting all this work
into it—for what?" he says
more to himself than to me,
as if he's sleep-talking.

"What do you mean *for what*?"
not sure what he's getting at—
and not liking it.

"It's just, I've got my real job too.
This isn't my job."

I shake my head in disbelief.
"You *weren't here* that night—
the night of the tornado, and we
needed you.
Mom
          and I
                    need you!"

"I'm sorry, Quinnie. I don't mean
to upset you. I'm just tired.
Dealing with the insurance
and all of this." He waves
his hand at our house.

"It's a lot. And . . . I don't know
if it's my house anymore."

I stare openmouthed,
no words coming out.

"Hey—forget it." He sits up.
"I've got something to show you.
Check this out." He holds his phone
and tilts the screen so I can see,
hits *Play*. "This is poetry for a good
cause," the reporter says. "An anonymous
poet with the pen name Nobody
will make you look. Make you pause.
The mural movement has been upon us
for years, but this is new—what looks like
graffiti is actually poetry."

The camera zooms in on a wall
that is more than familiar to me,
with sprayed-on words that read:

This storm story
will have a happy ending:
Neighbors helping.
Hearts mending.
          —Nobody

I almost shout *That's me!*
But keep my secret to myself.

"I thought you might like this,
since you're working on that poetry project.
Have you seen any of these?
I guess they've been popping up
around here since the tornado.
I kinda like this poet tagger guy."

I smile on the outside.

The inside of me
still struggling,
still reeling
from his words
about how it's not
his house anymore.

WORDS

Ms. Koval told me a writer's mission
is to find "the best word for the job."
You could say *sad* or *upset* or *thoughtful* or *pensive,*
but the word *melancholy,* according
to my friend the dictionary, means
all of these *at the exact same time*—
or *simultaneously.*

THE STORY OF A HOUSE PART II: AFTER THE STORM

"Home Sweet Home." People say these words when they arrive back to us. They sew, paint, and frame them. Lately, I don't feel it. My parts groan and creak. A chunk of my roof is missing, one of my walls is cracked, and my foundation may have shifted. Stormstruck! A near miss! But I am standing, and my people are just scattered. Some houses were not so lucky; they are bruised and beside themselves. Some are empty, lonely, whispering *No trespassing* to anyone wandering the dark streets. Why must we always be *sweet*? We could be *Home Melancholy Home. Home Embarrassed Home. Home Nostalgic Home. Home Resilient Home. Home Hopeful Home.* Maybe we are all of these behind our facades.

HANGING WITH MR. JONES

I hang again with my new besties,
Mr. Jones and Freddie,
in the fenced-in backyard.

We've gotten good at sharing
this place—me writing,
Mr. Jones piddling,
and Freddie snoozing.

"He slept like a baby"—

Mr. Jones points to Freddie—
"after you and my grandson took him
to the park the other day."

I've learned
this is
Mr. Jones–speak
for *Thanks*.

"When he was a puppy,
the missus and I used to take him
for a stroll"—Mr. Jones pauses,
stares off into space—
"but since the wreck,
my knees are shot."

I stop writing, scan his face
to read his emotions,
and make a mental note
to ask Ian about "the wreck."

POETRY PROJECT CONFERENCES

Conferences can't be private
in a class of twenty-five, with my back
to the class and a chair scooted up
to Ms. Koval's desk. She recently
moved Jack and Jade front

and center, to keep an eye
on them. They keep an eye on me,
tilt their heads to listen.

She begins, "I know the storm
kept you from submitting
some poems, but face it,
you're a poet now. No excuses."
Then she looks out at the class,
and back to me, leans forward,
gets serious, and whispers:
"Be who you are meant to be."

Jade coughs as I trip
back to my seat. "She's a poet—"
Jade looks to Jack "—and we
didn't even know it."

THE NOT-SO-HAPPY EVER AFTERS

After our conferences,
Ms. Koval discusses resolutions
and conclusions, how to leave
narratives open.

I stare at the notes I'm taking.
They blur out of focus
as I think about unhappy endings.

She explains how people
like things tidy, wrapped up neat
like a present, a "happily
ever after." "But life," she says,
"is unpredictable. Untidy. Surprising."

I look up at her.
I totally agree with that.
This eighth-grade year has been all three,
with Forrest departing,
the tornado descending,
Jack and Jade defriending
me, and my parents
back to waging war.

"Some writers," she says,
"let their readers' imaginations
finish the story, fill in the void
with their own interpretation."

I wonder about the voids
in my life's story
and if they're too deep
to be filled.

INSPECTION

"What did he say?" Mom asks,
as if Dad's answer doesn't matter.

They sit face-off style, several
feet apart, in the backyard
of Ivy. Something invisible
has permanently shifted
between
them.

"The foundation is a problem.
Perhaps it was before
the tornado. But we need more
support beams in the basement."
Dad sighs. "I'm just not sure it's worth
the investment it will take to fix—"

"—but we will make it livable,"
Mom completes his sentence.

He casts a sideways glance
in my direction.

"So, we're on the same page?" she insists.

"I guess," he says
under his breath—
but at a volume
for the three of us.

OLLIE OVER AND OUT
TO SOMEBODY I'M NOT

Like saying goodbye,
I walk to the skate park, where I spent
countless hours of my life,
and sit on the edge
        of the skate bowl, hang my legs over,
and watch the other skaters—
a five-year-old drops into the bowl and rolls
from shallow to deep end,
looking like a professional.
                Then slowly—it hits me
                along with a light breeze and a stab of loss
                but a new feeling of being grounded.
I don't have
        to master any of this,
and I walk away,
        wondering what
                I'm walking to.

THIRD-QUARTER REPORT CARD
FINALLY ARRIVES

A report card should not be allowed to arrive
at an address recently hit by a tornado—
especially if the grades are a storm themselves.
The grades are not up-to-date anyway.

A report card should not be allowed to enter
a mailbox hanging on for dear life
if the household cannot bear more bad news.
And parents should not be allowed to read
the report card if it might lead to another fight.
If you tossed it into a dumpster, the comments
would still speak volumes in your head:
Not performing up to her ability.
Doesn't turn work in on time.

THE ONE THING

In the backyard of Ivy, Freddie
rushes me, sniffs the damp report card
in my hands, and backs away, like he knows it stinks.
I sit in the grass, stare at ants carrying
heavy things on their back, and relate.
Freddie licks my face, as if to say,
"It's okay. I like you anyway."

"Sometimes he knows"—
Mr. Jones startles me—
"when a person needs cheering up."

I grin despite my grades.

"Something bothering you?"

"Besides my house being wrecked,
losing my best friend, never living
up to my brother's standards,
and living here? No offense."

"None taken." He actually smiles
as he rearranges his flowerpots,
plucks a weed growing in one.
"Some friends stay," he says, "others go.
But brothers are for life.

"You know, I had a sibling,
a twin as a matter of fact."

I notice his use of the past tense
and stare at him, imagining two of him.

"He was born bigger, happier,
better-looking, earned better grades too,
got a better job, and, he'd probably say,
a prettier wife."

I wait for the lesson, the *but*—

When he stays quiet,
I say, "But?"

"No buts. He was all those things.
Better all around than me."

Good lesson, good talk.

"But my wife loved *me,* not him.
Besides, that *stuff*
was important only to him.
The way I figure it, I had to find
my own joy—and I did. Took me
thirty years to figure that out."
He shakes his head and looks off
at the horizon as if he is stuck in a memory.
"All those 'better-thans' don't matter
if you find the one thing that makes you happy."

FOR GOOD, THIS TIME

Dad has pulled the bulk of his woodworking tools
from the basement and salvaged what he could from the shed.
His things are stacked in the middle of the dining room.

"Why are you gathering all your stuff?"
I follow him from room to room as he packs a stack of books
into a box, fills a backpack with his clothes and shoes.
He glances at me as if he's in pain, but I am the one in pain.

I don't let him out of my sight. In the bathroom, he packs
his toothbrush. "You could come *with* me," he says casually.

I'm caught off guard by his suggestion. "What about Mom?
And Forrest?" I ask through the tears I hadn't noticed on
my face. When he shrugs, I run out the front door.

I run
       all the way
              to Ivy,

where I find Freddie and Ian in the backyard.

Ian can tell I'm hurting
             and
       gives
            me space.

     I think he can also tell I need his company
because I can't talk, so he talks for us.

He talks about his grandma, Mrs. Jones.
"She was really cool, for a grandma."

I look up at him a couple times.

I even smile when he tells me
how they went strawberry picking every spring
when he was young. His grandparents in the front seat singing
and him in the back seat. How he came home red—
red fingers, red face, red arms,
red spots on his clothing,
red tongue.

After a while, he tells me about the wreck.
"Grandpa was always such a good driver," he says.
"It's what he did for a living—and he was good at it.
He's always blamed himself."

Then Ian says, "Things change.
I understand, Quinn.
It's hard."

Something comes over me.
"Do you want to see something?"
I don't wait for his answer. "Follow me!"
I lead Ian, Freddie leading us both,
around the block and through an alley
to my latest poem project.

Ian smiles and takes a picture.
He says, "Guess what?
I'm a nobody too. Matter of fact,
my whole school is filled with nobodies."

I laugh at a word
that might sound like a put-down
but right now
sounds like a club
I want to belong to.

A JOURNAL

Before class ends today,
as if she knows I need something,
Ms. Koval hands me a journal.
It's the softest leather,
the color of a grocery bag,
with crisp lined paper
and a little strap to tie it shut.
When I look from it to my spiral
only half full, she says,
"I just thought you might like it."

I open it on the bus, touch
the gift of blank pages,
and begin to write. Jack
and Jade scoot a seat closer,
all laughs and caffeinated energy.

A woman gets up and moves
away from their bodies
in constant motion.

"Didn't get it all done
in your new study hall?"
Jade says, more to Jack
than to me.

I shake my head, ignore,
and keep writing.

"Writing about us?" she asks.

"Why would I do that?"
I close the journal.
Tie it shut.

"Oh—are we not interesting enough?"

In a flash, Jade bends over the bench
and snatches the journal from my lap.

"Let me see." She yanks it open
and pretends to read. "Look, Jack!
She's writing *in* her journal
about her journal. Deep!"

I don't reply. I don't even try
to snag the journal back.
I stare at Jack, pissed.

Jack looks bored, looks back
down at his phone.

"Nothing to say to us?" Jade continues.
"You got plenty of words
to write." She opens the window
and dangles the journal out
by its little strap.

I lurch forward, reaching
for her arm. "You're the worst!"

"I'm just playing,"
Jade snorts.

Jack adds, "It's a joke, Quinnie," then stifles
a yawn and looks away from the two of us.
"Quit. Give it back," he tells Jade.

Jade looks disappointed but tosses
the journal back at me.

I stare them down for a second,
my breath ragged and my chest heaving.
On an impulse, I toss it out myself,
doing what Jade couldn't.
Proving I don't care.

The payoff is instant—
Jack's grin is huge, like he used
to give me all the time,
back when . . .

MORE LOST THAN FOUND

I jog-run back
to the approximate scene of the crime,

trying not to picture Ms. Koval's eyes
when she gave it to me, in an *I believe in you*
kind of moment.

Mom and Dad are too busy
with their jobs, the house, and their marriage
to tell me they believe
in me, but I'm sure
they do.

I can't believe I tossed the journal!

On my hands and knees, I search
the ditch and comb through grass
and weeds along the street.

When I can't
                  find it,
                            I walk to City Park,
empty-handed and heavy-hearted,
pull my old spiral from my backpack,
and write down all I can remember—
but most of the words
are lost.

"A REAL BEAUTY"

A man on a bench
nearby is also writing.

Maybe he lost something too.
He glances my way and says,
"She was a real beauty."
He points at a sideways tree,
one of many toppled in the park.
"Yeah," I agree, wondering
if he's a poet, like me.

A team of chainsaws
arrive and scatter
birds and squirrels
from their home,
begin to disassemble it.

The tree I once fell asleep in,
one of City Park's oldest,
now also lies horizontal,
a casualty,
a body down.

THIS FIGHT IS STAGED AT IVY

We all have our roles.
Mom is yelling.
Dad is yelling.
I play the idiot,
openly crying.
I don't know the cause

of this fight—
I wonder if *they* know.
I listen for clues.
Is it about my grades?
I follow them
like a stage director,
from kitchen to bedroom,
back to kitchen, fixing
items disrupted in their path,
and closing windows,
to keep this rehearsal
to ourselves.

TAKING A BREATHER

I can't
resist
the urge
to be close
when they argue,
like I must witness
what occurs, because
if I'm good enough, maybe
I can stop it. But I can't stay calm
this time, as they spiral.
I step outside to catch my breath
and of course—

      Ian is standing there.

He looks at me
with stupid, kind eyes,
so I know he's heard.
I want to crawl in a hole.
I want to be gone.
I want to disappear.
My face speaks shame
in hues on my cheeks and neck.
I don't wait for his words, my grip
on this world tips and reels,
so I run. I run away from Ian,
out of the yard,
away from Ivy,
away from them,
away from my life—
as it is currently
written.

THE OVERPASS

Just last summer,
the three of us stood right here.
Each a foot shorter.
We counted cars—
an innocent game.
I took red. Jack blue. Jade green.
We guessed their speeds
and watched the blue lights

as someone got pulled over.
I recall, we rooted
for the officer!

But tonight,
Jack and Jade allow me
back into their pack,
and on the way there,
Jack picks up a chunk
of concrete from a debris pile
next to the bridge. Junk is everywhere—
our poststorm toys. Jade laughs
and hefts a piece into her shirt.
They look at me.
And wait.

It's a turning point.
A moment I know will lead
to no good, but it doesn't seem to matter
what I do. I can never be
good enough.

I pick a bigger piece
and hoist it above my head.
Just like them.

We carry them to the overpass,
hold them in our hands like power,
like freedom, like the answer to everything we feel
but don't understand.

I drop the concrete
onto the bridge when the weight
becomes too much, and watch it
scatter into infinite pieces,
shooting outward at our feet.

Then I lean over the bridge
and spit, a tiny droplet of me disappearing.
I imagine it hitting a windshield.
Jack and Jade drop their concrete
and do the same.

After a while,
it's not enough to fix whatever
we're feeling, and Jack picks a piece
of the concrete back up.

"Are we going to do this or what?"
he shouts to the world—
and to Jade and me.

It never entered my brain
          what he was thinking of doing
                    until that moment.
Maybe that's when it struck him too.

He throws a baseball-sized chunk
                              over the bridge,

and we run to the bridge's railing
to see it smash onto the interstate—between cars.

A blue car swerves to miss it.

Jade yells, "Yes!"
I turn to them
in silent shock.

Jade has already picked up
another rock.

All of a sudden,
I am not okay with this.
I may not be perfect, but I'm not this
either.

"Stop!" I yell.
I try to pull the rock from Jade's hands.
She shoulder-bumps me away,
and I land on my butt.

"Seriously, Quinnie?" Jack stares,
unimpressed.

"This could kill someone," I plead,
my voice rising, tears forming,

heart banging.

When Jack picks up a piece of concrete,
I yell, "I'm leaving."

"Fine. Go home, Quinnie.
You're hardly ever here,
and we don't miss you
when you're gone," Jack says.

Jade covers her mouth, like Jack scored big.
"Yeah, go write your poems," she adds.

I take several steps backward,
away from them, away from the sting
of Jack's words, stumbling
on my own two feet
and the hurt.

Then I turn
and bail.

I'm not running
to put words on paper,
or to spray-paint them—
but to speak them.

BAILING

I run away
as fast as I can,
tears blinding my eyes.

Words save lives.
Words save lives.
Words save lives,
I repeat in my head
with each step I take.

Mr. Jones's words.

I think of words
in my hands instead
of concrete.
Something I can use.
For something good.

My feet, one
in front of the other,
direct me
past apartments
past bus stops.
I run across a crosswalk.
That's when I spot
a police car parked
at the dollar store.

I run to the window
of the seated officer.

JUVENILE DETENTION CENTER

I hear from my parents,
who got a call from Jade's parents,
that they were taken
to the Juvenile Detention Center
and may be facing CRIMINAL
mischief charges.

We sit stiffly in chairs
in the kitchenette of Ivy.
Mom and Dad look at me
with eyes I've never seen.
They tell me an officer
saw Jade and Jack throw
a rock from the bridge.
They storm me with questions,
probably assume
I threw them too.

They ask why I was
hanging out with them,
if they were doing that.

I try to explain how I left—

but they don't listen
as well as I'd like.

Dad tells me he's proud
of me, thinks I did the right thing,
even if it doesn't feel good.
"You may have saved a life."

Mom cuts him a *shut up* look,
and I know this is
the freewrite to a fight.

Mom lectures,
"This stuff is not fun and games.
Someone could have died."

Dad nods solemnly.
I agree quietly.

"There's been a lot going on,"
Dad says more to Mom than me,
"since the tornado. I'm sorry
we haven't been here more."
Dad gives me a look of apology.

When he leaves,
Mom tells me I'm grounded.

I nod. It's my fault

my friends got caught.
It was the right thing.
And it was hard.
It will cost me.

FINALLY BACK IN OUR HOUSE—GROUNDED AND ALONE

Mom and I
move back into the "Nash Family House."
She's in her bedroom, door closed.
On my bed, I sit.
Alone.

After all this time,
I found my phone in my laundry basket—
and it works, after a good charge—
but I'm grounded from it
unless it's an emergency.
I think of calling Jack,
asking him to forgive me.
Isn't saving a friendship
an emergency?

Our friendship is
a jumble of memories,
snapshots, sounds, and images.
Skateboards slapping concrete.

Rumble of road beneath our feet.
And before that, the two of us
on birthday bikes, tag in yards,
lunches in the cafeteria,
bare feet in damp grass at dusk.
The greeting he uses only for me—
"What's new, Q?"—and my reply,
"'Sup, Jack?" And his two-word
response, "Good talk."

This year, his voice
has been rough with change,
but it's still more familiar
than my own. And now,
his voice is gone.

In one memory,
he taunts me to climb higher
in an oak tree in the park, his face
through branches dappled
in light, glowing like love.
And I climb toward him,
as he climbs higher
and higher.

THE STORY OF A HOUSE PART III

People say *If these walls could talk,* but would you really want to
hear from me, your house? I might tell you, "Get out of bed, quit

your moping—whatever you're dealing with can't be that bad."
I might tell you that houses are more than walls, ceilings, floors,
and doors, that families breathe life into us and move through
us like blood through a heart. People also say *Home is where the
heart is.* But sometimes people pack their stuff, drive away, and
never come back. And do you really want to hear that? I might
tell you that hearts can change—and when that happens, *you*
have to change too—and it's hard.

MIDDLE SCHOOL IS ABOUT OUTGROWING

I've outgrown things:
three bikes, toys, clothes, and shoes.
I outgrew every pair of pants
I owned last summer.
I had a favorite shirt, baby blue.
Now it's too short, too tight.
Either it shrunk or I grew.
I outgrew the habit
of sucking my thumb,
but it took six years.
I outgrew a toddler bed,
my first skateboard,
a fear of shots and the dark
in my bedroom at night.
But what happens when you
outgrow a friend?

MY NEWFOUND FEAR OF STORMS (AND BEING FRIENDLESS)

Dad says, "It's PTSD," how you think
differently before and after something traumatic.

Post-Traumatic Stress Disorder

Like when I was bitten by a dog
and I didn't trust them afterward.
That's why I used to shoo Freddie, although
I've learned he's harmless—and I've grown attached.
Before Forrest left and after, the door
closing behind him. When Dad was living at home again,
and now that he's at Grandma Jo's for good.
Before the tornado and after.
Eighth grade feels like living in the before,
before my future begins—and the terrible waiting
like the heavy air before a storm.
Dad is on the phone with me now,
because Mom isn't home and I have no friends,
and there's a "severe thunderstorm warning,"
which I now consider an emergency. The winds
are picking up and the sky is bruised. My legs shake,
my hands shake, my voice shakes as I hold the phone
sitting on the top stair of our basement,
in our repaired home. He's talking me through it.
"I'll always be here—" but he's literally not.

Then he says, "I'm sorry this is so hard."
And I know he means more than the storm.

A HORSE OFF HIS ROCKER

From home to school
from school to home,
I leave
return
depart
arrive.
There are few places
I'm not grounded from.
And in between the two,
I meet a horse
        stalled in an alley
midstride, paused
on his broken rocker—
raring to go anywhere
but here, where he and his rider
are separated forever.

Trudging past,
I run into Mr. Jones
on a rare walk
with Freddie. I think:
What about your knees?

Old me would've looked away,
turned up a different alley.
New me smiles
and says, "Hello,
Mr. Jones!"

"I'm afraid you spoiled him," he says,
and nods at Freddie,
who pulls Mr. Jones
right up to me.
Freddie is so wiggle-wild
it's almost embarrassing,
but he inspires me:

"Thank you, Mr. Jones,
for letting my mom and me stay with you—
and for your story—about words
saving lives."

Mr. Jones nods again,
clears his throat, like
he's at a loss
for words.

SPRING DOES ITS THING ANYWAY

as if Nature didn't get the message
that events have been called off, delayed,
Easter egg hunts canceled due to yards filled

with hidden shards, shingles, and nails.
I pause to capture and describe it in my spiral
as I wander from one street to another.

I discover a house with no second floor
yet bushes of reds and yellows and a tree
in full bloom leaning against its chimney,
and its front door open wide in welcoming.

On another lot, rows of tulips and jonquils
line the sidewalk, oblivious. The owners
planted them to accent a house now gone,
a rectangular pit where the basement sat.

Nature keeps throwing her own little party,
regardless of the state of her guests.
She brings colorful gifts—
and the promise of future storms.

THE BIG ANNOUNCEMENT

Ms. Koval clears her voice,
prepares to announce
the readers for the eighth-grade
May poetry reading. I sit
on my hands so they won't shake
and betray me, and my cheeks
burn lava-hot.

"I'm waiting," she says, stands statue-still,
her cue for us to close our mouths,
click *Pause* on our conversations.
She's mostly talking to Jade, who's talking
to Jamari, who's talking to Jack—
none of whom are talking to me.

I consider the POV poems
I've written and my growing portfolio
and cross my fingers under my desk,
hope to hear my name,
as if it's my last shot
at becoming something.

Ms. Koval begins.

"Kiera.

Jamison."

A smattering of claps and snaps.

She continues.

"Lochlan.

Thomas.

Lance."

I don't dare look anywhere
so I don't catch anyone celebrating
that I'm not chosen—

"—And Quinnie,"
she finishes.

I look across the room,
notice Jack smirking at Jade,
who's palm-planted her head,
and catch him saying the most hateful
thing he's ever said.

"I can't come to the reading," I blurt out,
without raising my hand.
"There's a community fundraiser
that night in my neighborhood."

I swallow back a sob.

Ms. Koval nods.
"Oh! That's certainly important."

When the bell rings,
I dash to the bathroom,
where I lock myself in a stall
filled with mean graffiti
and let the tears fall.

PITY PARTY

I invite no one but myself.
No guests, no food, no décor.
No friends, since I have none.
I sit alone in my bedroom,
staring at the door.
I miss Freddie and Mr. Jones—
even though they're just down the road.
I should be grateful.
Ms. Koval called my name.
My house is restored.
My bedroom is redone.
Mom and Dad are okay—
just split up & divorcing.
Maybe I didn't want
to read my poetry anyway.
Maybe reading poetry out loud
to a crowd isn't my thing.
Maybe THIS is a pathetic
excuse for a party.

FUNDRAISER FOR A FAMILY

I feel bad for lying to Ms. Koval,
who has only ever treated me kindly.
The fundraiser, which is really tonight—
not the night of the reading—

is the *one* event I'm allowed
to attend. It's in support of a family
whose house got severely damaged.
They're serving pizza in their front yard,
and there's a donation jar. I've brought
twenty from my savings to give them.

Since I don't know anyone, I gravitate
toward a table supplied with paper
and crayons, where a little girl is coloring.

I sit down beside her. "Whatcha making?"

She holds up her picture. "It's my house,
once Mommy and Daddy fix it." She's made it
prettier in the picture. I doodle a poem
about her house and share it with her.

A small crowd has gathered around.
A woman overhears me reading
and adds fifty to the donation jar.

She asks me for my poem. Stunned,
I hand it over.

She tells me to sign it,
so I think on it for a full minute,
then make a decision
and sign it *Quinn.*

Word spreads I'm penning poems
because the lady is a talker and a sharer.
I sell three more, and the little girl
sells a picture. Together, we earn big bucks
for the happily-ever-after of her house.

"FOLLOW YOUR HEART"

Mom holds her phone
and mouths, "It's Forrest," to me.
I would rather disappear
than hear another Forrest success story
of the week, but when she hands
over her phone, he sounds unlike
my upbeat brother.

I carry the phone upstairs.

He's cramming for exams,
and still has to pack his dorm
and write three essays and turn in
his books. He confides he's burnt out
and thinking of taking a gap year.
He even apologizes for not
emailing me back to check in.
I can't believe my ears.

I tell him to *Hang in there!*
or some other quotable
Hallmark-ian nonsense.

"Take my advice," he sighs,
"have more fun than I did in high school."

"It's hard to have fun while
grounded," I tell him, but take a chance
and confide in him about the reading,
and how I haven't asked Mom
since Dad left.

"That sounds important, Quinnie.
She'd totally un-ground you for that.
The fights aren't about you.
You know that, right?"

"I guess so."

"I know so. Also,
you should totally follow your heart
to that art school
you mentioned in your email."

Which, I think, means
Forrest might have actually read
the poems I sent.

But I don't take a chance yet—
and ask about that.

SYNONYMOUS

Mom labels them *Disagreements*.
Their lawyer says, "Irreconcilable differences."
I still call them fights.

The details are pointless.

But for once,
I wonder
if maybe this fight is *not* about me—
not about my grades
and *not* about my former friends.
Writing my words is helping
me understand my feelings
and suddenly I wonder
if most of their fights
have *never* really been
about me.

AN APOLOGY

Later, Mom finds me (writing) in my bedroom.
"You have a poetry reading, Quinn?"

I look down at my spiral.

"Talk to me," she says gently.

"It's no big deal."

She turns her phone off, pockets it,
and sits down on my bed to listen.

"I can't make all As like Forrest, Mom,
but this is something
I *can* do."

"I'm so sorry, Quinn,
if I made you feel like
I wanted you to be like Forrest.
I want you to be yourself—and
I'm proud of you."

Tears fill my eyes.

"And . . . I was too harsh on you.
I was preoccupied and scared—
and I don't think I got it, until your dad
made me hear him. I know
you did the right thing with Jack—
and it's been hard."

My vision blurs—and though
I can't see her clearly, it's like
she's really seeing me.

I fall forward into her arms
and she sits still
and holds me.

"ON ONE CONDITION"

I stand in front
of Ms. Koval's desk.
I think she knows
why I'm here
before I speak.

Luckily,
she doesn't quiz me
about the conflict
I claimed to have
with the reading.
She just listens,
which is what
I love about her
as a teacher—
and person.

"This reading

means everything
to me. I have things
I want to say
with my poetry—
and I hope
you will still
allow me
to read."

I'm surprised
when she says,
"Of course."

I take a huge breath,
relax my shoulders—
then she says,
"On one condition."

I think of my slightly
improved grades
in other classes.

"I expect you
to submit your portfolio
to Turner School
of the Arts."

What?!

My eyes are full moons.
She has more confidence in me
than I do—maybe more than anyone does.
And then, she says the magical words
that singsong themselves
in my head longer
than I'd like to admit:
"You're a natural poet, Quinnie."

THE END-OF-THE-YEAR EIGHTH-GRADE POETRY READING

I am all nerves and jitters.
Whoever metaphor-ed it
butterflies got it wrong.
It's definitely baby
hippos trampolining
in my stomach.

The lights are dimmed, and the chairs
are arranged in a semicircle.
The principal sits front and center
in her white suit and heels.
The parent organization is selling
snacks and drinks, with a homemade
sign that reads *Coffeehouse*.

I pull Mom to the first chair I find.
Then we see Dad already seated

on the other side of the library, on his phone.
Soon enough, Mom is on her phone too.

Before I can suggest we move,
Ms. Koval turns off the music playing
quietly and snares everyone's attention.
She tells us to stow our devices
and introduces the evening's program.
Ms. Koval's voice quivers, and I realize
she's nervous too.

I think of what she said
about no one being an island—
and I want to remind her of this, but I can't,
so I give her a big smile, which she sees,
and gives me one right back.

She says some other things,
but I cannot hear them
because my heart starts
pounding in my ears.
I try to pay attention
to the other readers.

But THEN
I spot Jack—

   What's he doing here?

at the snack table.

He sees me and looks away,
finds a seat as far from us
as possible, but still I feel
a tiny blossom of hope
in my chest.

Kiera is reading a poem about her cat.
After her, it's Thomas, Lance,
and then me. Between the readers,
parents and students applaud
and snap politely.

When it's my turn,
I know Ms. Koval has said my name,
but I am glued to my seat.
Jack casts a quick glance my way.
Ms. Koval fills the silence by telling
the audience that I'm applying
to the arts high school for writing.
Mom looks surprised and squeezes
my shoulder, whispers, "You got this!"
This gets my legs working.

Somehow, I make my way
to the mic, look down at the poem I chose.
Perhaps not my strongest, but one
I need to read, one I've committed
to memory. I fold the paper in half
and take a deep breath.

"LEARNING TO FALL"
BY QUINN NASH

I clear my voice,
see a few heads pop up
when I say Quinn.
I glance at Jack,
at Mom and Dad,
and then begin:

> A friend once told me
> "you have to *learn* to fall"
> when I was attempting
> a skate trick I couldn't master.
> He said, "Stand up, dust off,
> go again—but fall better."
> At first, I shrugged it off.
> I've been learning my
> whole life about falling,
> which is a type of failing.
> Nothing new. But he said,
> "Falling correctly prevents injury,
> so you don't break an arm,
> a leg, a wrist, or worse."
>
> I've failed lots: math tests
> especially, and friendships too.
> The problem is—
> in life when you fall, you may

save yourself, you may even save
someone else, but there's always
injury. Not broken bones,
but hurt just the same.
Maybe learning to fall is about
getting up and dusting off
when things don't work out.

When I started writing this,
I still thought my friend
would be my friend again
if I could just succeed
at all the things we shared.
But his success and mine
are two different paths—
and we're both going to fall
along the way, more than once.
Everyone falls. It's how
you get up and go again
that matters most.

Writing and calling myself
a poet is the biggest trick
I've ever attempted—and I
don't plan to bail on it.
But along the way, I will think
of my friend and say his
five words to myself:
Just fall better this time.

OVATION

After I stumble through
the final lines, when I look up at the audience,
I cannot find Jack anywhere.

      He must have left as soon as I started.
I am teary, even as the room cheers and claps
and my parents and Ms. Koval give me
a standing ovation.

PORTFOLIO

After the reading, Mom and Dad unite
briefly to ask Ms. Koval some questions.

"With your permission," she explains,
"I can help Quinnie—I mean Quinn—complete
her application. It will be late, but she has a shot.
She's put a lot of effort into her schoolwork
and writing these last few weeks."

Mom and Dad can't thank her enough.

"Quinn is talented, and I couldn't be happier
to write her a letter of recommendation."

I'm surprised to hear this,
since I turn work in late more than on time,

and since I haven't always stood up for her
in the classroom, when it's been
Koval vs. the Students.

She and I spend the next week editing
and revising and arranging my portfolio.

When I hit SUBMIT just in time, I'm a shipwreck,
my heart trying to sink like the *Titanic*
but hoping to float like a lifeboat.
(I can't stop writing and thinking
and dreaming in similes and metaphors.)

Ms. Koval smiles.
"Now we wait."

LIFE, ACCORDING TO ME, QUINN

It's like the two roads poem.
Life is one big fat choice.
Dad asks me to come live with him.
So I must choose between parents,
between houses, between schools.
I'd say between friends, but I'm short
on those these days.

Right now, before high school,
I choose Quinn over Quinnie—and Quinn
over Quinn(ie) from now on, and not

because of Mom, but because it's who
I've always been inside. I'm escaping
the parentheses in my family.

Don't let life tell you who you are.
I don't have to be the best, like Forrest.
I just have to be me. And I'm enough.
Choose a path—and do what it takes
to walk it, even when it hurts.

FORREST IN THE CITY—BRIEFLY

College is out, so Forrest is driving toward us.
He's already scrapped the gap year idea
and landed an internship in DC, but he'll claim
his space in the spotlight at home for a few days.

I'm imagining family game and movie nights
during the week he's home, but Mom yanks me
back to reality when she mentions that he'll stay
with us for half the week and at Grandma Jo's
with Dad the other half. Out of habit, I had
envisioned the four of us around the table.

It's still hard to comprehend the math.
A family of four divided by divorce equals
two in one house at the same time—
and sometimes three.

MY NEW AND IMPROVED BEDROOM

I stare at the poem from the reading
Mom framed and hung on my wall.
She also made me a writing nook
in the window, so I can look out
at the new dogwood Dad planted.
She stocked my desk with pencils
and a bag of gummy bears.

When Forrest arrives, Mom's at work,
so he dashes upstairs to find me.
"Quinnie!" He hugs me and attempts
to swing me around like he used to.
I am momentarily a planet
revolving around his brightness.

"I'm going by just Quinn now," I tell him
when he sets me down.

"Cool," he says without a second thought.
"Look at this place! Is this where you write?" he asks—
and before I have time to answer, "You know,
I mostly wrote to look good for my college apps.
Seems like you're the real writer of the family."

That's when I know he's read my poems.
Maybe, just maybe, I haven't been
seeing him through a clear lens either.

I give him a tour of the restored house.
"It's better than before," he says.

"I guess." I shrug. "Just different."

"Yeah, Mom and Dad." He nods
in understanding. "You've been through a lot."

I sit down beside him on the couch.
"You used to think *I* was the reason."

"For what?" he asks, looking confused.

"For them splitting up."

"I never thought that."

"You said it once—or thrice."
I stare at my hands in my lap.

"I'm sorry—if I said that. I was stupid,
or jealous. Who knows what I was thinking!
They've been unhappy for so long, Quinnie—
uh, Quinn. It was just a matter of time.
I'm sorry it happened
with you home alone."

THINK-PAIR-SHARE

Jack and I come face-to-face
in English class. Ms. Koval partners us
for an end-of-year "Think, Pair, Share."
We're supposed to discuss something
we've learned this year about ourselves
and one goal we have for high school.

Jack and I bypass the script and wing it.

"What's new, Q?"

"'Sup, Jack?"

"Well, at the reading, I learned
you're a poet now."

"I thought you didn't hear me read?"

"Nope, I was there."

"Oh!" I say, surprised,
and, "Sorry I missed your birthday."

"So, am I the friend in your poem?"

"Of course." I allow a grin.

He nods. "Good poem."

"Thanks." I pause.
"Jack, I hope you don't
hate me for the rock thing.
I'm sorry for what happened
afterward."

"About that—"
He pulls a crumpled piece of paper
from behind his back.
"Don't read this till later."

"Ohh-kay," I say, and fold
it neatly and pocket it.

"Start to wrap up your talk," Ms. Koval
nudges the classroom. "Prepare to share
one thing your partner said."

She always does this—a random
sampling—to see if we're
really listening to each other.

Jack raises his hand
before she calls on anyone.

"Yes, Jack?"

"Quinn over here
is going to keep writing
poetry in high school—
and probably become
a world-famous poet.
You can all say
you knew her when . . ."

He smiles in my direction.

"Thanks, Jack," Ms. Koval says.
"You're a good listener."

TRANSITIONS

before
        during
                after—

Ms. Koval taught us
to add transition words to our writing
with this ^ to make our thoughts flow.
Not as easy to add them to life.

Jack will always be
my childhood best friend.
But I've changed,
and so has our friendship.

In just a few short months,
I've moved from feeling like a big zero,
from Quinn(ie), a wannabe skater,
to a pretty good poet.
Before and after.

Tornados happen.
So does divorce. But there's
a lot more to do with choices—with doing.
Volunteering and helping my neighborhood,
with writing—that's when I saw myself clearly.
That's when I became
who I'm going to be.

ACCEPTANCE

The letter finally arrives
in our repaired mailbox.
Mom and I hold it between us,
staring at the formal envelope.
We're sitting on the porch swing,
our favorite new place to be—
together, a spot where we
can wave to Rashad or the Wests.
We swing back and forth,
and the house sings
a creaking, hopeful song.

We are pleased to inform you that you
have been accepted to Turner School of the Arts,
to study in the Writing Conservatory.

We stare at it
and reread those words
about ten times.

And it feels
like acceptance.

COURAGEOUS INTO SUMMER

I am in the park journaling,
across the street from Ivy,
listing things I've learned this season:

I have a talent for writing.
I enjoy helping others.
There's room for more than one
success in a family.

But things will happen—
forces of nature
that are not your fault.

I spy Ian's mom pulling into the driveway of Ivy.
I haven't been back to visit Mr. Jones

since we moved,
since the reading,
since Forrest coming home.

I close my journal
and walk over, hopeful.
Ian's in the backyard,
with a couple suitcases surrounding him.
Freddie sees me and tries to leap the fence.

"Hey there!" I say.

"Hey there!" Ian returns.

I let myself in and pull up a chair
beside him. "Guess what?"

"What?"

"I got into Turner!"

Joy starts in his eyes
and takes over his face.

"You'll be a sophomore,
and I'll be a freshman," I say.

"True," he says. "Congratulations, Quinn!
I didn't know you applied."

"Yeah, well, you're the reason
I knew about the school.
Thanks for that!"

He smiles,
        and then a different emotion crosses his face.

Freddie goes to the back door and whimpers.

"What's all this?" I point to the suitcases.

"Mom and Dad are moving Grandpa into a home."

My eyes go wide and I am wordless.

"I know," he says, and looks down.
Freddie comes over and licks his knee.

Ian rubs Freddie's head. "Good boy.
He's been a mess."

Freddie whimpers again,
tail between his legs.

"What happened?" I ask.

"He took a minor fall on the stairs
and they thought it would be safer, better,
and closer to our apartment."

"What about Ivy Manor? What about Freddie?"

"I don't know. Dogs aren't allowed where we live."

I stare at him, unsure how to help.
I was just writing about
how you can't always help,
even when you really, really want to.

Ms. Koval has taught me
that listening is often
the best gift.

Without saying anything,
I lean toward him and touch his hand.
He opens his hand and I put mine into his.

"I'm here if you wanna talk," I say.

He struggles to keep
his mouth from trembling.

And then, something comes over me,
and I lean forward and kiss his sad mouth.

After, he cannot form words.
Finally, he manages, "Maybe you can
come visit Grandpa with me sometime?"

"I'd like that."

AN UNEXPECTED GIFT

A couple days later,
Mom and I are on the porch swing
when Ian walks by with Freddie
on a leash. Mom waves them over.
Ian sits and tells us the updates
about Mr. Jones, who's settling in
to his new home. "He doesn't hate it,
but he misses this guy." He rubs
Freddie's neck. "Mom is thinking
of putting an ad out to find him
a new owner."

"You know," Mom says, thinking,
"maybe we could keep him.
Then you could take him
to visit your grandfather
whenever you want."

Ian practically jumps off the porch.
"I know my grandpa would want Quinn to have him—
I just didn't want to ask."

I look from Mom to Ian,
my smile increasing in size.

It had not crossed my mind—
because of my old fear of dogs—

that I could be a dog owner.
"Well, he's no Pumpkin," I say,
"but I could get used to him."
Freddie comes over and licks my face.

I look up at Ian and we lock eyes,
knowing we're both thinking
about the kiss.

"QUINN SAYS"

"Let's play a game,"
I tell Freddie.

"Quinn says *Sit.*"
Freddie sits.

"Quinn says *Down.*"
Freddie lies down.

"Quinn says *Good boy.*"
Freddie wiggles and waggles,
like I've always been
his home.

REBUILDING

Dad drops by.
Asks if I want to take a walk.

We leash Freddie and set off.

We plan to walk the route we walked
the day after the tornado.

The neighborhood has come a long way
in a little over two months. But there are blue tarps
over roofs still, empty lots, houses sitting untouched
and in various stages of rebuild. We pass
the house where I helped the woman find her cat,
Peevie. We pass the firehouse—they've straightened
the flagpole. We pass the house with the fundraiser,
and their work is almost complete.
The little girl is playing in the front yard.
I wave at her, and she waves back.

I show Dad three of my poems
on our walk. He is amazed it was me
all along and takes pictures of them—
"nature and art coming together."

"I'm not surprised you're creative," he laughs.
"You take after your dad.
Are you still going to skate?"

"Just for fun. What are *you*
building these days?" I ask.

"I thought I'd build this guy a doghouse.
Just got some good cedar I can use."

"He'd like that. He loves to be in our backyard,
now that the fence is back up."

We walk Freddie to the dog park.
I step in this time, braving the mix.
We unleash him, and he runs wild
with the other dogs.

He partners with a yellow dog
circling the park. Chasing.
Leaping. Barking.

Finally, the yellow dog runs
to locate its owner, and I'm totally shocked
to find out it's the one and only Ms. Koval—
in a summer skirt, T-shirt,
and ponytail.

"Well, hello there!" she says.

"Hi, Ms. Koval. Is this your dog?"

"Just adopted him. Meet Diogie," she says.
"Get it? *D-O-G*?" She slowly spells out each letter.

I laugh at her teacherly name for her dog.
"I'm a dog owner now too.
Old dog, new trick!" I smile sheepishly.

"Hello, Mr. Nash." She greets Dad.

"Hope you're enjoying your summer," he says.

Our dogs run off together
while I tell her all about getting into Turner,
and before we leave, we make another
dog date to meet at the park.

"Ms. Koval, thank you.
For believing in me
and helping me get into Turner.
It meant everything."

"That's what teachers do," she says.
"Besides, your writing got you in."

THE STORY OF A HOUSE: THE NEXT CHAPTER

I know now
the story of my house
is also the story of me—Quinn.
I think of Ivy Manor too,
where I met Freddy and Ian,

where Mr. and Mrs. Jones
lived together all those years.
I think of the houses
in my neighborhood.
Maybe the story of a house
is the story of people
and families coming and going,
and growing and changing,
of wrecks and divorces and tornados.
My family does not live
together in one house now.
And I am not the same person
I was before. People say
home is where the heart is—
but it's more complex than that
when the *where* is spread between
places. And one day, I will not
live in *this* house anymore.
Maybe the story of a house
is simply the story
of relationships.

      Before school let out,
Jack gave me something he'd written.
A poem he wrote after my reading,
although he said it wasn't a poem.
It was about my house—and how
when his dad left him and his mom,
my house became his home.

He doesn't say it, but I know
it made him feel
like he belonged.

"JUST TOYS"
BY JACK EDWARDS

We were at your house,
maybe it was a Saturday
or a summer of Saturdays,
and we were building our future
out of Legos—the streets,
buildings, our houses and cars.
We named our city
Jackquinnville, and it was
ours. We peopled it.
Even then, you gave us stories,
gave us jobs and families,
made them up with words.
I remember your mom
brought us Goldfish and we
fought about what color
to build the courthouse. You
wanted yellow. I'm sorry
I insisted on red. We turned
our toys into wishes and dreams.
I remember how you looked
at my house and said:

"You can bring your family
to visit mine anytime, and I'll
bring mine to visit yours."
I know they were just toys,
and we were just kids, and
who knows where we'll end
up, but thank you,
Quinn, for being
my best friend.

ODE TO A TORNADO

Is it weird to write a poem
for a storm? I think I'm okay
with weird. I'm headed off
to art school, after all.

Thank you for bringing
Mr. Jones, Ian, and Freddie
into my life. Thank you
for showing me that helping
my neighbors feels good.

You taught me to slow down,
to tune in, to observe, to write,
to think, to choose, to appreciate.

You showed me my talents.
You changed me.
You scarred my home—
but in some ways
I am stronger.
I am more
than before.

WRITING

In my nook,
a picture of my family
balanced on my windowsill,
the sapling dogwood below,
pencils sharpened and new journal
ready, I position the Lego girl
atop a piece of rubble
I found in our yard
a month after the tornado.
I take a deep breath,
close my eyes, and wait
for my ideas
to show up
word
by
word—
and they do:

THE GREAT ADVENTURE

Moonglow through
a window. I am all energy.
Night-struck. Awake. Tiny explorer.
in the darkness of my rehome,
I trust my paws to lead
the way through man-made
tunnels. Whiskers working,
guiding, nose wiggling.
The scents are safe. I run
the wheel. Pause to observe
and listen. Sniff the clean,
full bowls. Unsure what
comes next—I scurry
onward in curiosity,
burrow in fresh chips,
groom myself. I am no
longer Pumpkin. My new
friend has named
me Lucky—
and I am.

ACKNOWLEDGMENTS

Thank you to my two big-hearted readers: friend and fellow writer, Heather Hale, and my mom, Rebecca Brooks. Heather, our writing alliance is five-star; thanks for talking books with me while steering clear of alligators on your walks. I'm holding you to that retreat celebration for your first book. Mom, thanks for reading *literally* everything I write and for your bouquets of story ideas.

Thank you, Richard, for your spaghetti and meatballs (it never gets old), endless coffee, and forever love. Without you, what would I do? Rosabelle and Rowan, thanks for love and support, while I try to mom, write, and teach—my attention forever sliced and divided like a pie. You are my everything!

Midsouth SCBWI chapter, you seriously rock, and I'm eternally grateful.

Thank you, Louise Fury, my agent and book champion, and to the entire amazing Bent Agency.

Mikyung Lee—your stunning artwork absolutely sings.

Thank you, Sally Morgridge, my brilliant editor, for turning my doc into a story. Shout out to the hardworking Holiday House crew, especially Derek Stordahl and Mary Cash. Kerry Martin, thanks for making beautiful books. Thank you, Barbara

Perris, for correcting my malaprops, and Laura Kincaid, for your attention to detail. I cannot thank the HH publicity and marketing team enough: Terry Borzumato-Greenberg, Michelle Montague, Sara DiSalvo, Aleah Gornbein, Mary Joyce Perry, Elyse Vincenty, Alison Tarnofsky, Darby Guinn, Mary Wolford, and Annie Rosenbladt.

East Nashville is where I've nested, raised children, and found kinship—from soup groups to writing groups to friends made across yards and at Shelby. My East Nashville years, also, have been impacted by natural disasters. We moved to East Nashville soon after a 1998 EF3 tornado hit the area. In 2010, a 1,000-year flood wreaked havoc. Then in the early hours of March 3, 2020, mere days before COVID-19 would change how many of us live and work, East Nashville was struck by another EF3 tornado. At the time, it was one of the costliest tornados in United States history. In that 2020 devastating outbreak of EF3 and EF4 tornados in west and middle Tennessee, lives were changed and lost. Thank you to the first responders, community groups, and volunteers who came when we needed you. In the aftermath, the neighborhood united, sharing stories and scars, lending a hand and an ear, and rebuilding hope from heartbreak. Thank you to my neighbors for allowing me to tell a story inspired by you!